Lock Down Publications and Ca$h
Presents

THE REAL BADDIES OF CHI-RAQ

VOLUME 1

Written By
KING RIO

First Edition 2024

Printed in the United States of America

This is a work of fiction. Names, characters, places, and incidents either are products of the author's imagination or are used fictitiously. Any similarity to actual events or locales or persons, living or dead, is entirely coincidental.

Lock Down Publications
P.O. Box 944
Stockbridge, GA 30281
www.lockdownpublications.com

Like our page on Facebook: Lock Down Publications
www.facebook.com/lockdownpublications.ldp

Stay Connected with Us!

Text **LOCKDOWN** to 22828 to stay up-to-date with new releases, sneak peaks, contests and more…

Like our page on Facebook:
Lock Down Publications

Join Lock Down Publications/The New Era Reading Group

Visit our website:
www.lockdownpublications.com

Follow us on Instagram:
Lock Down Publications

Email Us: We want to hear from you!

PROLOGUE
Unexpected Blessings, Nefarious Intentions

"My apologies for interrupting your night. I sent for you two because I got gifts for the both of you. A girl's best friend, you might call it. Cost me an arm and a leg."

Princess gasped at Weezy's words. She loved diamonds. As Weezy slid open his desk drawer and carefully removed two, foot-long gift-wrapped boxes, Aqua and Princess shrieked in unison, interlocking their manicured fingers under their chins. They stood at the opposite side of Weezy's large oak desk, both dressed in thong underwear and six-inch stiletto heels, their perfect breasts exposed to the cool breeze blowing down from the air vents in the ceiling.

The two women, both twenty-two, were strippers at Queen of Diamonds, the newest and largest strip club in the city of Chicago. With more than forty thousand square feet of floor space, including a main floor, a second floor where twenty private rooms and Weezy's office were located, and a third level that housed the training center and an industrial-sized kitchen. QOD was the *"it"* spot of the moment. The club had opened for business just over ten months ago and already it had been name-dropped in Jeremih's latest club banger. Kevin Gates had recently used the venue to throw a bachelor party for an elite member of his entourage. MBM Young Meach and CMG's GloRilla had shot a music video on the main floor. Chicago Bulls power forward Malachi Mitchell and sixteen of his friends were currently in the spacious, roped-off V.I.P. section, popping gold bottles of champagne and raining thousands of dollars on the beautiful

4

exotic dancers in celebration of the five-year contract he'd just signed for a guaranteed $160 million.

"Y'all helped me turn this club into what I always knew it could be," Weezy said. He reached across the desk with both gift-wrapped boxes balanced on the palm of one massive hand. He gave one to Princess, the other to Aqua.

The girls quickly ripped off the wrapping paper and flipped open the lids of the black velvet boxes.

"Ahhh!" Aqua shrieked. She jumped up and down, and her surgically fattened butt cheeks made a clapping sound as she did it. "Oh, my God. Thank you so much!"

Princess took her Cuban-link necklace out of the box and gawked at all the twinkling white diamonds. There was a pendant, too. It read *PRINCESS* in white VVS-quality diamonds.

Weezy got up from his black leather swivel chair and walked around his desk to stand behind the girls and help them put on their necklaces. At 6'9" tall, he towered over the two young women. Aqua was 5'2", and Princess was 5' 5" with her spiked Louboutin heels bringing her height to a respectable 5'11" but Weezy was still a giant behind them. His head was bald, his skin as dark as his wide, intelligent brown eyes. He smelled of some masculine cologne that possessed light notes of tobacco and citrus. His finely tailored three-piece Stefano Ricci business suit was dark blue in color. The expensive fabric stretched snugly around all his rolling slabs of muscle.

Aqua had always been attracted to tall black men. Weezy's fingertips grazed the nape of her neck as he linked the necklace together. His touch ignited a fire deep in her loins that spread through her sexy diminutive body like a raging California wildfire and turned her nipples to stone.

"Altogether," Weezy said, his low baritone voice overflowing with unbridled arrogance. "I paid over two hundred thousand dollars for these. Had Johnny Dang make 'em. This kind of ice puts you on another level. This puts you next level. Only millionaires can afford to drip like this."

Aqua voiced another enthusiastic thank you, and Princess voiced one a few seconds later. Stroking the man's big ego was common practice at Queen of Diamonds. Those who didn't bow down were soon replaced by new dancers who would wrestle with a tiger for a chance to rake in the big bucks at Weezy's hot new strip joint.

"It's nothin' to me, you know," Weezy continued, linking the necklace for Princess now. "I mean, I blow through a quarter million online gambling every week. Bet y'all can't name another man who's blown two hundred thou' on you at once. Maybe over time, but not all in one whop."

He returned to his chair and sat down. Leaned back, admiring the two half-naked beauties standing before him, his eyes lingered on their breasts, on their meaty thighs, on their sloping Coke-bottle hips, and then his gaze shifted to his open desk drawer. He reached down into it a second time. His big hands came out with two large rubber-banded bundles of cash. All hundreds by the looks of it.

Princess narrowed her eyelids at Weezy. He placed the two rubber-banded piles of hundred-dollar bills on his desk and kicked his drawer shut, moved forward in his chair, adjusting the knot in his blue silk necktie. "Here's another hundred grand. Fifty for you and fifty for you. Spend it as you please."

"What's the catch?" Princess blurted out. She couldn't restrain herself from asking it. There was something lurking under the murky waters of Weezy's kind gestures. Something dark and sinister. She could feel it in her gut, festering there like undigested pork flesh. Aqua gave Princess a hard side-eye.

"No catch at all," Weezy said rather quickly. "Just an appreciation for all the high-end clientele you two have brought to this establishment. Most of these guys come here to see Princess and Aqua. Everybody knows it. No sense in not awarding it." He picked up the cash and tossed one bundle to Princess and the other to Aqua. "I also went ahead and switched you both from Preferred Shift to Prime Shift, so you'll be able to maximize your potential. You'll start your new shifts tomorrow."

"Oh, my God," Aqua murmured. Tears shimmered along her lower eyelids. She fanned her pretty face with splayed fingers, hyperventilating. "I don't know what to say."

"A simple thank you will suffice," Weezy said, as if she hadn't thanked him twice already.

Princess fought off the urge to roll her eyes as Aqua uttered another thank you. Weezy nodded his head and extended a hand toward the door, permitting them to leave. His smile showcased two rows of perfectly white veneers. It was a forced smile, Princess thought. He was wearing it just for them.

Walking out behind Aqua, Princess turned to pull the door shut and shot one last glance at Weezy, fully expecting to find him staring at her fat bouncy ass. What she saw surprised her. Weezy's gaze was distant, and he looked...worried. He had picked up his smartphone and was holding it screen-up in the palm of his hand, but he was staring above and beyond it, at a spot on the gold-veined marble wall across the room from him.

Princess hesitated. She was tempted to ask Weezy what was on his mind. But she was topless and half-dressed, and she didn't want to get fined fifty dollars and chewed out by the House Mom for being late to the stage for the second time this week, so she pulled the door shut. Her mind reeled with questions as she and Aqua sauntered down the long hallway, passing the spacious private dance rooms on their left and right as they approached the two elevators at the far end of the hall. In the wall to the left was a third elevator marked *Employees Only.* It descended straight down to the locker room Princess shared with seventy-two other full-time QOD dancers and a few dozen freelancers. To the right of the two main elevators was an office roughly a third the size of Weezy's. Through the wide glass window Princess could see the tow brawny bouncers, Bobby and Tank, sitting behind their long wooden table, their focus on the camera monitors in front of them. They were watching live feeds of the private rooms. The cameras were unable to record and save footage. *At least that's what Weezy told the girls*, and sex for pay was not uncommon. The bouncers were the eyes in the sky, there to watch over the dancers and keep them safe from unruly customers.

Princess and Aqua entered the *Employees Only* elevator. They waved at the bouncers as the door slid shut. Tank waved back as he shouted out. "Bling, bling! Let me borrow a couple dollars." He had a crush on Princess, and usually she entertained his advances. Right now, though, she was too preoccupied with trying to figure out the motive behind Weezy's sudden acts of kindness.

Something was wrong. Of this, Princess was certain. She was also certain that her close friend and former roommate, Talisha 'Aqua' Mason, was far too carefree and optimistic to see through the bullshit.

"Welp," Aqua said, thumbing away her tears of joy and holding up her impressive mound of cash, "Now we got more than enough to buy that rental property you wanted to go half on, and I can get Mama's roof fixed. I was just praying for a blessing to take care of all that this morning and look at what fell in my lap. God is good."

Princess nodded and said nothing. She too was grateful for the blessing. She'd been having trouble with the brakes and air-conditioning in her E-class Mercedes, and the costs of maintenance for the German-made luxury sedan were through the roof, but she was pretty sure this particular blessing had not come from the good Man upstairs.

Weezy snapped out of his troubled reverie the moment Princess pulled his office door shut. He looked down at his iPhone and sighed defeatedly. "There're gone," he said.

The man on the other end of the line was eighty-year old Herbert Harris. Weezy had put him on speakerphone before the girls walked in, and Herb had muted his end to keep the girls unaware of his presence.

"Good." Herb's gravelly old voice was low and heavy. "Give them a week to enjoy themselves. Then, next Friday, have them meet you at GAM's for lunch. That's where I want you to be when we give them the details of the first hit. We'll sweeten the offer by giving them a hundred thousand dollars apiece this time on me."

"Princess won't do it. I'm telling you. She's too…"

"Don't fucking tell me what Princess won't do! You'll make her do it or else! Understand that?" Herb waited, breathing hard enough for every breath to be heard through the speaker. When Weezy didn't reply, Herb went on. "You owe me, Roy. If you want out of this, you'll get those pretty little stripper bitches to do exactly as I say, with no questions or idiotic opinions. Are we clear on that?"

Weezy balled his right hand into a fist and slammed it down on his desk so hard that his computer monitor nearly tipped over. From his desktop computer he could access all sixty-eight cameras inside of QOD and the two dozen cameras outside, but right now he was focused solely on the split-screen view of the two camera feeds blown up before him: the strippers' locker room area, and the adjoining 2,300 square foot health and fitness spa where for a small fee of $160 a month, the exotic dancers could exercise, shower, receive relaxing massages, consult with medical professionals, and practice their sexy dance moves away from the prying eyes of the strip club patrons.

Weezy had a sneaky suspicion that one of his employees was in cahoots with Herb. How else could Herb have known to pick Princess and Aqua for the job, two dancers who were close friends and had lived together in the same apartment? If Herb didn't have a dancer working with him, then it had to be a bouncer who knew the girls personally, or a DJ. Maybe even the House Mom.

"Listen, Herb, I wanna get all this shit done and over with just as bad as you. All I'm saying is that you picked two of the worst girls for this kinda work. I got a hundred other bad bitches we can choose from, some real treacherous bitches who live for this kinda shit. Aqua's a good girl. She wouldn't hurt a fly, and Princess is too street smart. Doesn't listen to anybody. She'll turn that money down and walk away from this. I'm telling you what I know."

"Then it sounds like you have some serious ass-kissing to do. One week." Herb hung up, and for a long while Weezy sat watching the camera feeds. He zoomed in on Princess and Aqua as the two incredibly beautiful, young black women strutted out of the elevator and into the locker room. All the other girls looked towards them, no doubt wondering why the two friends had just returned from the boss's office wearing brand-new diamond necklaces and holding rubber-banded stacks of hundred-dollar bills. About fifteen of their fellow dancers closed in on them as they went to their lockers. The rest of the girls who were either dressing themselves at their own lockers or sitting in front of the well-lit mirrors in the dressing room area getting their hair and makeup in order turned their heads to stare at Princess and Aqua. Several hands reached out to touch and admire the sparkling Cuban-link necklaces and pendants.

"He makes me spend over three-hundred thousand dollars on these two young hoes," forty-year-old Roy "Weezy" Sullivan muttered aloud to himself. "No matter what I say to persuade him to pick two other girls, he absolutely demands that we use Princess and Aqua." Weezy began stroking his heavy beard as he continued his soliloquy. "I'll figure all this out, Herb. And when I do, you're a dead man. You and whoever else it is you got working with you."

Chapter 1

"I know I better see some goddamn lap dances in the next two goddamn minutes…" Weezy's deep voice boomed from the loudspeaker that was positioned just below the high-tech Panneton security camera, and the girls went scrambling. Princess lost sight of Aqua as they stashed the cash in their lockers and joined the frantic line of exotic dancers rushing out to meet customers.

This was what the House Mom's schedule referred to as the Preferred Shift. It ran from 6:00 p.m. to midnight and was one of the more sought-after shifts, especially on the weekends. The Prime Shift, considered the most coveted shift of all ran from 10:00 p.m. to 2:00 a.m. The big spenders knew that Prime Shift was the best time to see the baddest bitches on QOD's roster perform on stage. All the club's most popular dancers- Cherish Taylor, whose stage name was her real name, Shmoney Rose, Thick Doll, Sasha the Stallion, Kimmy Kakes, and Bunny XXX performed only on Prime Shift. They'd become so well-known for it that people had started calling them PTG, short for Prime Time Girls.

The time was 9:45 p.m. and the club was filled to near capacity. There were dope boys and scammers, jack boys, and boosters, business owners and nine-to-fivers. A few high-rollers and celebrities occupied the VIP section, which was roped off and glassed in, accessible only by climbing one of the spiral staircases that led up to a second level overlooking the main stage.

Princess found her mark at a table near the bar: a handsome young black man sporting lightly tinted Cartier sunglasses, thickly corded dreads that hung down past his shoulders, and a mouthful of diamond teeth. He wore a red Balenciaga jogger with matching sneakers, and like Princess he wore a diamond flooded Cuban-link necklace. His pendant read *40th & Blvd.* A Cuban-link bracelet the same width as his necklace graced his gaunt right wrist, and an iced-out Rolex Sky Dweller watch that encircled his other one. The four men seated with him looked older. They had several tall piles of one-dollar bills stacked neatly together on their table.

"Welcome to Queen of Diamonds. I'm Princess. Can I interest you in a lap dance?"

"Hell yeah. What's the ticket?"

"Twenty for a lap dance. Fifty for a private dance in one of the Blue Rooms upstairs."

"Shit, I came all the way from Nap Town to see yo' sexy ass." His voice was low and smooth, barely audible above the bass heavy Lil Durk song the DJ was playing. He dug in his pants pocket and dragged out a folded wad of hundreds. Peeled off two of them. "I'll tip you a hundred for two of those private dances. Oh, and I'm Small Body, by the way. My hood niggas call me Bodies."

A hint of a smirk raised one corner of Princess pretty mouth. "Follow me," she said, taking the two hundreds and tucking them behind the string of her thong.

Small Body trailed her to the elevator doors. When the two of them were alone in the elevators, she looked at his reflection and caught him gazing wantonly at her fat round derriere. He reached out as if to grab a handful of it and stopped just shy of her skin, his big diamond chompers sinking down into his full bottom lip. Princess decided she liked him. He was a bit shorter than the men she was used to dating, maybe 5'8", and he couldn't weigh more than a buck fifty, but he looked good. He smelled good, and he exuded a certain confidence that Princess found to be both attractive and intriguing.

"You got big teeth," she said, grinning.

"And you got a fat ass," he retorted.

"You like it."

"You a'ight." He smiled. "You ain't no Beyonce."

"So, you mean to tell me you drove all the way from Indianapolis to Chicago for a girl who's just a'ight'?"

His smile grew until she could see all twenty of his diamond teeth. He adjusted his necklace and twisted his diamond pinkie ring to the left and right. Tilted his head to one side and looked at her backside while she watched his reflection on the chromium steel door in front of them.

"Okay," he said finally. "I'm cappin'. You bad as fuck, but you already know that. I been in your DM's for the past four or five months and you ain't even read my messages. Had to show my face to get some attention."

"No," Princess corrected as the reflective door slid open before them. "You had to show Benjamin Franklin's face to get some attention. Now come on. Let me show you what all this ass can do."

Chapter 2

Aqua reached high above her head, took the pole in both hands, and lifted herself off the stage floor as she went into a slow, seductive spin. Flipping herself upside down, she spread her legs and shook them, then closed her legs and made her big yellow butt cheeks wiggle and clap before flipping right side up and sliding down the pole. She hit the stage floor in an ass jiggling split.

Young Meach, The Grammy-nominated gangster rap artist who'd risen to fame under the tutelage of trap music superstar Blake "Bulletface" King, was performing onstage behind Aqua. While holding the mic to his mouth with one brilliantly bejeweled brown hand, he used the other to thumb hundreds off the stack of cash he held over Aqua's head. The crisp new bills rained down all around her, while more than thirty others surrounding the stage applauded Aqua's exotic dance moves and showered her with handfuls of one-dollar bills.

Headliners like Bulletface only performed during Prime Shift, and only Prime Shift girls performed onstage with headliners. This rule usually irritated Aqua to no end, especially when the headliners was someone like Chris Brown or Trey Songz. Now, though, Aqua was excited about the rule, she was still a Preferred Shift girl tonight, but tomorrow, when H-Town's hot girl Megan Thee Stallion hit the stage to perform all the hits from her latest album, Aqua would be onstage with her.

14

Aqua stood up, her small delicate hands clasped around the pole in front of her as she bent forward and bounced her ass against Young Meach's cash stuffed Louis Vuitton sweatpants. Her eyes swept the crowd. She saw dozens of regulars and hundreds more new faces. A line of ten sexy bottle girls marched up the spiral staircase to VIP, each girl holding up two gold bottles of Ace of Spades champagne. The bottles had sparklers attached to them, making a spectacle of the moment. Aqua figured the bottles were likely headed to the Bulls player's section, since it was well-know that Bulletface only drank Lean, and she wondered how much money the dancers up there were making.

Doing another slow spin around the pole and whipping her thirty-inch-long mop of fiery red braids over her shoulder, Aqua turned her back to the pole and pulled up one side of her red Gucci thong, sticking her notably long tongue out between her teeth and smiling around as Young Meach gaped at the bulge her thick vaginal lips made in the crotch of her panties. He stumbled over his lyrics and chuckled at his mishap. Several people in the crowd laughed.

"I feel you, bruh," a tall, pot-bellied man shouted from the crowd. "That lil bitch is bad as fuck. I would've stuttered too."

Aqua was used to men being at a loss for words when they laid eyes on her. She was a bad little mulatto girl, a yellow bone with a pretty face, a small waist, and a huge round ass that measured forty-four inches around. She'd inherited her mother's deep dimples and juicy, full-lipped smile. Her doe-like eyes came from Stevie, her father, who'd been sent away to prison for drug trafficking seven years ago. She had piercings all over, from her tongue and her left nostril to her nipples and clitoris. Her stomach was as flat as an ironing board, her waist just twenty-four inches, making her waist-to-hip ratio visually appealing enough to stop traffic every time she went out in public. She'd lived a relatively sheltered life in the Chicago suburb of Joliet before her father was sent away, and she had made good use of all the alone time she spent at home, gaining a loyal social media following first for her unprecedented beauty and expert makeup tutorials and then her provocative lingerie shoots and Cardi B inspired twerk videos. She'd accumulated close to a million Instagram followers before she ever even considered dancing professionally. The simple truth was that she loved putting all her lovely lady curves on full display, especially to the droves of men and women who followed her on TikTok and IG to fawn over her beauty. She absolutely craved the attention. Her boyfriend, Day-Day and the four boyfriends before him had broken up with her after looking through her direct messages and finding that she'd been messaging dozens of other men throughout their relationship, many of whom flooded her inbox with absurd sexual requests, marriage proposals, cash, and gift offers. Many of which she accepted, and unsolicited dick pics, among other things.

Day-Day was Davion Carroll, a 6'7" shooting guard for the Dallas Mavericks. Originally from the westside Chicago neighborhood of K-Town. He and several of the Conservative Vice Lords he'd grown up with were somewhere in the building. Aqua had seen them earlier, sitting together at two side-by-side tables, drinking and eating hot wings and talking.

Aqua executed a fast spin around the pole and lifted her cherry red Gucci stilettos off the cash strewn stage floor, scissoring her lusciously meaty legs in front of her. She was searching the crowd for Day-Day, wanting him to see her impressive new moves, when she observed Prime Time Girls making their highly anticipated entrance.

They came in through the front doors with Bunny XXX leading the pack in a pink colored mink coat that was open just enough to reveal the skintight pink Fendi print minidress and hot pink open toe heels she wore beneath it. Bunny XXX idolized the famous urban model Bernice Burgos because a lot of people said they looked alike, but Aqua thought Bunny looked more like Princess than Bernice, only Princess was a lot thicker, a few shades darker, and a few commas poorer. Bunny XXX, the only QOD dancer who was also an adult film star, had an estimated net worth of $2.7 million.

The entire PTG squad wore high-end fashion and gaudy diamond jewelry; Weezy had gifted them their Cuban-links and name pendants months ago, and as a rule the girls only dated millionaires who could afford to keep their massive walk-in closets filled with top-of-the-line designer fashion. As the Prime Time Girls strode arrogantly through the crowd, escorted by eight hulking bouncers, people raised their phones to snap photos and capture video of them passing by. Aqua knew that they were about to pass through the dressing/locker room area and into the adjoining health and fitness spa, where they had their own private locker room next door to the House Mom's office. Their locker room had larger lockers, sumptuous red leather scfas, a spacious bathroom, two eighty-inch smart TV's, and even a rear exit that opened to the parking lot. They'd only entered through the front of the club to make their royal presence known. One corner of Aqua's wetly glossed red lips curled upward in a thoughtful smirk as she continued her dance onstage. *"Tomorrow,"* she thought elatedly. *"Just one more day and I'll be one of them."*

"I owe you big time, Weezy," Aqua muttered under her breath.

When Young Meach completed his fifteen-minute set, Aqua used a rake to gather all the cash on the stage into a single pile before the next scheduled dancer was called out. Johnny, a tall, coal black bouncer who'd suffered a gunshot wound to the hip some years ago that left him with a distinct limp, snapped open a black trash bag and held it open for her as she scooped up and dumped in all the dollars.

She went through the towering blue sequined curtains at the rear of the stage and into the dimly lit marble-floored hallway that opened into the locker room's southwest corner. As soon as she pushed the curtain aside she ran into Tasha, a 6'1" Amazon with rich chocolate skin, striking blue eyes, and a whole lot of ass. Tasha eyes widen when she saw Aqua like a frightened deer caught in the headlights of a speeding eighteen-wheeler.

"What?" Aqua said, stopping and planting a hand on her hip. "What the hell you looking at me like that for?"

"Oh, uhhm…it's nothing." Tasha shook her head. "I'm up next, that's all. I always get nervous before I go onstage.

"Mmm hmm." Narrowing her eyes at the tall woman, Aqua decided to push the giant's suspicious reaction to the back of her mind. She started to walk past Tasha, but Tasha reached back and grabbed her by the wrist. Aqua looked back over her shoulder.

"Hold on," Tasha said. "I have to tell you this."

"Tell me what?"

"It's that bitch Shmoney Rose."

"What about her?"

"I don't know. I guess she's mad about you and Princess being switched to Prime Shift. She said nobody told her about it. Big Gabby said she didn't even know about it, and she's the House Mom. Anyway, Shmoney Rose is pissed. She's, uhm…well she just had your…" Tasha trailed off.

"Spit it out. She just had my what?" Aqua pressed.

But Tasha only shook her head and sighed and mumbled something about it being none of her business. The podium host called Tasha Blaze to the stage. She turned and disappeared through the ruffled blue curtains, leaving Aqua alone in the hallway with nothing but her own disrupted thoughts to keep her company.

Chapter 3

"So how much you chargin'?"

Princess tilted her head to the side and wrinkled her brow in confusion, staring down at Small Body as he pulled out his bank roll of hundreds and began thumbing through them. He was seated on the blue leather upholstered sofa that ran along two walls of Blue Room number four in an L-shape. There was a pole in the middle of the blue carpeted floor, blue light bulbs embedded in the smooth blue walls, and a camera just above the door that could see every inch of the room. Aside from a small blue trash can in one corner, the room was empty.

Princess had shown out on Small Body's lap, as evidenced by the protruding tent of erection at the front of his joggers. She'd quietly admonished him for repeatedly breaking the club's *"no touching"* rule, but he hadn't listened. His eager little hands wandered all over her body. He peeled loose five hundreds and offered them to her.

"What's that, a tip?" Princess asked.

"Nah. Hell nah. I'm tryna fuck. My nigga said y'all be sellin' pussy up here in the private rooms, just like them hoes at Arnie's."

Princess's pretty mouth fell open in surprise. She stared blankly at Small Body for a long silent moment, waiting for him to crack a twinkling diamond smile, to say he was only joking. Then her face tightened, her teeth clenched, and her nostrils flared.

"Look nigga," she snapped. "I ain't no fuckin' prostitute. I might show off my body and pop my pussy to pay my bills, but I only fuck my man. If you wanna fuck me, you have to date me. I don't do sex on the first date either. Some of these other bitches in here might sell their souls and everything else, but I don't."

"A'ight, a'ight." Body raised his hands in surrender. "Damn, my bad."

"Damn right, it's your bad. And even if I was a prostitute, five hundred dollars wouldn't even get you a hand job."

"Will you calm down?" Body spoke calmly and grinned with amusement.

"I bet you done had every STD in the book. What, you ain't got no game? The only way you can get some pussy from a bad bitch is by paying for it. Hmm?"

Small Body chuckled and shook his head, stuffing his bank roll back in his pockets. "I said I'm sorry. Look, just hear me out. I drove almost three hours from Indianapolis just to see you. I message you every other day on IG, comment on all your pictures and videos, and you don't even reply to my messages. Don't get me wrong, I understand it. Shit, you got a million other people following you on there, so I know you got thousands of unread messages. That's why I told my nigga Stikks before I left the hood that if I couldn't get you to be my bitch, I would at least try to get one night with you, at whatever the cost. Now I apologize if you take that the wrong way, but that's...that's just what it is."

Princess grew quiet, holding her hips and breathing nasally, realizing she had overreached and lost her temper. Having exerted a lot of her energy during the two-song lap dance, she was hot and sweaty. Thin rivulets of perspiration snaked down her neck and in between the perky swells of her C-cup breasts. She studied Small Body's solemn expression and decided she wasn't mad at him after all. His rather unorthodox explanation for coming at her the way he had was actually the most romantic thing she'd heard in a long time. She smirked and rolled her lashy brown eyes.

"So, what that mean? We got a date?" Bodies smiled like an infant, his eyes wide and hopeful.

Princess extended her hand, palm up. "Give me your phone."

He handed it over quickly, as if he feared the iPhone might spontaneously combust if he didn't get it out of his possession right then. Princess accessed his text messages and spent twenty seconds nosily strolling thought them before composing a one-word message and sending it to her own cell phone.

"Here." She gave back his phone. "I'll text you sometime tomorrow."

Bodies looked at the text message she'd sent to her phone. "Ruler? What that mean?"

Princess moved forward and straddled Small Body's lap, resting her forearms on his shoulders. She felt his erection between her thighs, long and hard, throbbing against her.

"Well," she said, "it feels to me you got about twelve inches down there like a ruler. And if you act right on our first couple of dates, you might just get lucky to use it."

Chapter 4

Big Gabby was an exceptionally large woman, about as heavyset as Lizzo, her favorite pop star. Although she was nowhere near as wealthy as the flute playing young songstress, she certainly had more financial stability than most black women in Chicago. Every dancer at QOD was required to pay her twenty dollars when they tipped out at the end of their shifts. It was compensation for her maintaining their schedules, keeping their restroom stocked with all the necessary toiletries, providing sexy outfits for the girls who didn't bring their own, and closely reviewing their attendance, appearance, demeanor, and customer service. In order to dance at QOD, each dancer was first required to audition in front of Big Gabby, and she alone was responsible for the hiring and shift assignments.

Which is why she was in a rage about Princess and Aqua being promoted to Prime Shift without her approval. Weezy had never dipped his nose in her affairs before, and he wasn't about to start doing it now. She barged into his office and found him pacing a tight circle behind his desk. On his face was a look she'd never seen on him before, a malevolent mixture of fire and ice, his eyes burning hot, his snarl freezing cold. His fists were balled tight, his footfalls hard and thunderous. His blazing eyes flashed toward Gabby, and she sucked in a deep breath without even meaning to.

"You in on this shit?" Weezy barked.

"Oh, no. Hell no. Don't you dare try to turn this around on me." Big Gabby snapped, slamming his door shut as she stepped inside. "You switched Princess and Aqua to Prime Shift without even consulting with me. Since when did we start doing that? Because apparently I didn't get the memo."

Weezy stopped pacing. He stood there looking at Big Gabby, glaring at her from seven feet away, a hellish conflagration burning hot behind his unwavering gaze. Beads of sweat trickled down from atop his smooth bald head. His two-thousand-dollar shirt was half open, his suit jacket tossed haphazardly over the back of his swivel chair. An open bottle of Hennessy stood next to his computer monitor. Its contents half consumed.

"If I find out you're working with him…" Weezy crossed the room in two long strides.

If his footfalls were like thunder, his speed was like lightning. His enormous black hands moved almost too fast for the human eye to see. One hand clamped around Gabby's neck, sinking into the excess fat and squeezing, while the palm of his other hand came down hard across the side of her face.

"I'm killing you first. On my brother's grave. I'm killing you right in front of that old-ass nigga and then I'm killing him."

The coppery taste of blood filled Big Gabby's mouth. Her vision blurred. Her left ear rang like a church bell, and the diamond Chanel earring she wore in that earlobe fell to her shoulder and tumbled to the floor. All of the courage and anger she'd possessed mere seconds earlier melted away. Fear replaced those emotions, a deep guttural fear that her life was suddenly in very serious danger.

The moment of violence was fleeting, ending as shockingly fast as it began; the sight of red liquid shimmering between Gabby's thin lips seemed to douse the flames behind his eyes. He released his suffocating hold on her neck. Turned and strode back to his desk. Plopped down in his chair and sat back with his eyes fixed on the high ceiling above.

"You...you hit me," Big Gabby said shakily. She struggled to hold back the tears as she squatted low in her stretchy turquoise Chanel bandage dress and picked up her costly diamond earring. "You hit me, Weezy."

"I apologize," he muttered, not sounding genuine at all. He ran his hand down his face and shook his head despondently. "I'm sorry, big baby. I shouldn't have put my hands on you. It's just that I'm going through so much bullshit right now, and to know that I got somebody in my own circle working against me, that shit got me heated. I ain't gon' lie. On Larry."

Big Gabby moved forward on wobbly legs. The tears fell free of her hurt brown eyes and created twin trails of moisture on her dark round face, but she didn't sob. She picked a tissue from the Kleenex box on Weezy's desk and wiped the tears from her fleshy cheeks, then the blood from between her lips. She ran her tongue along the inside of her left cheek and felt the bleeding laceration, and it was at that precise moment that she began to hate Roy Sullivan. He'd been a grimy, scheming, verbally abusive tyrant of a business owner from the day she first met him four years and two months ago, back when he'd hired her as the regional manager of his three McDonald's restaurants, but this marked the first time his abuse actually turned physical.

Her pudgy brown hands became furious fists at her sides; she'd been holding her iPhone in her right hand, and now her adrenaline-fueled death grip threatened to break it in two.

"You black ass son of a bitch," she said through firmly clenched teeth. "You had better had a great fucking explanation as to why you just slapped me like that, something I can really fucking process, or I'm taking you straight to federal court and suing you for every red cent you got. And I do mean all of it. The legitimately taxed millions, and the untaxed millions you got from selling dope to those boys in Englewood."

Slowly, one degree at a time, Weezy turned his head to look at Big Gabby. He stared at her for five impossibly long seconds, the fire gradually rekindling, the glacial scowl returning with a vengeance.

"I got an eighty-year-old man tryna extort me. He got me on video doing some shit I shouldn't have been doing, some shit I could've easily paid somebody else to do. I offered him a million dollars cash to end the shit, but he wouldn't take it. Said he already got money. He's the one who made me switch Princess and Aqua to Prime Shift. He wants me to use them to set up the Vice Lords."

Big Gabby squinted at Weezy and tilted her head to the side. She was beyond enraged, but the fact remained that Weezy was the sole reason she had become a millionaire at thirty-five. She lived in a South condo worth $1.9 million. Her eighteen-year-old son Blitz and a few more of her close relatives resided in a suburban Illinois mansion she'd purchased for $2.1 million. She and her aunt Crystal were the co-owners of *Whips Out*, a burgeoning lingerie line worth $1.5 million, and Gabby was the sole owner of two Arby's restaurants in Des Plaines and Joliet, Illinois. She drove to work every day in a 2024 Porshe Taycan Turbo, and she'd gifted Blitz a brand-new Jaguar F-Pace when he got his license last year. None of that would have been possible without the thousands of dollars she got from the QOD dancers, and no matter how angry Weezy made her, losing out on that lovely four thousand dollars a night income was not an option. She lowered her head to the garbage can beside Weezy's desk and spit out the blood that had accumulated beneath her pierced tongue. She trashed the bloody tissue and crossed her flabby arms over her massive G-cup tits.

"Okay," she said, still squinting. "You got my attention. Tell me what's on the video."

Chapter 5

Shmoney Rose pushed her wet pink tongue out between her pearly white teeth and bit down on it as Davion Carroll penetrated her pussy with two long fingers and used his lips to kiss and pull on her stiffly aroused clitoris.

You smell so good down here," he said, looking up at her. "Like some fresh fruit or some'n."

Twenty-four-year-old Tiara 'Shmoney Rose' Moore smiled down at Day-Day's handsome walnut brown face and combed her fingers through his neatly groomed dreads as he went back to sucking and licking on her most sensitive erogenous zone. He was sending electric jolts through the nerve endings and causing her back to arch involuntarily. She had her long thick legs pulled back so far that the seven-inch heels of her white leather knee-high Jimmy Choo boots were touching the door panel behind her head. She was lying on her back in the backseat of her hot pink Bentley Bentayga, nearly folded in half against the rear passenger's side door as Day-Day exercised his tongue on her pussy. She'd had him take off his shirt. She'd sucked his nipples, kissed on his abs, and deep throated his dick until his salty warm gushes of semen clogged up the back of her throat. Now his dick was hard again, and she couldn't wait to feel it deep in her stomach. She pulled him up, kissed him on the mouth, added some tongue and tasted herself on his lips. She ran her hands over his powerful chest, admiring the tattoos that covered him from waist to neck.

"You are so fucking fine," she said, nibbling at the corner of her lower lip. "I don't know what your girl was thinking. I would've never cheated on you."

"I ain't got no condoms." Day-Day rubbed the head of his dick up and down between the slippery folds of her pussy.

"Just don't cum in me. Pull out and shoot in my mouth." Shmoney Rose reached down to help guide him in, and she gasped as the thick girth of his hard brown dick stretched her wide and deep.

Sliding in and out of her, first with just the top three or four inches of his significant length, and then with the next few inches, Day-Day's light brown eyes perused her flawless feminine curves. Standing at 5'7" with the astonishing shapely measurements of 34C-26-45 and a smooth peanut butter complexion, she was by far one of the most beautiful black women Chicago's Auburn Gresham neighborhood had ever birthed and certainly one of the top five baddest bitches to ever work the stage at *Queen of Diamonds*. A bevy of red roses and tulips were inked into the skin of her left leg, spanning from the outside of her knee up to her fat round buttock. She had full, succulent lips. She wore faux eyelashes; sharp, gel-manicured fingernails, and pinkish red iKiss Kosmetics lip gloss. The diamond flooded Cuban-link she wore around her slender neck had an attached name pendant spelling out *Shmoney Rose* in white VVS diamonds with a red and green diamond rose stretched across the lower part of the cursive lettering. Her necklace was notably slimmer than the ones Weezy had given to Princess and Aqua. In fact, Princess and Aqua's necklaces were larger than the ones Weezy had gifted all the Prime Time Girls. The pendant a few inches smaller.

It was the general consensus that their necklaces were cheaper than the ones Weezy had given to Princess and Aqua that had all the rest of the Prime Shift dancers feeling some type of way. Shmoney cast her eyes downward, looking past the disappointingly inferior necklace. Her spirits were immediately brightened by the sight of Day-Day's glistening wet penis as he plunged into her firmly gripping vagina. Her juices coated it from end to end. Day-Day's dick was by Shmoney's estimate roughly ten inches in length, and it had a slight upward curve that did wonders to her G-spot. She used her fingertips to massage her clitoris in slow circles and moaned like a porn star, resting the back of her head on the door, squeezing her eyes shut.

"This gon' be my pussy from now on," Day-day said. He kissed her on the mouth, shoved her dark pink Ivy Park shirt up over her bra-less breasts and mashed them together as he licked and sucked on her rigid nipples.

There were no pendants hanging down from his four diamond necklaces, but they were made of decent sized round white diamonds that probably cost five times the price of Shmoney Rose's Cuban-link, and the diamond Patek Philippe watch on his left wrist was worth at least a few hundred grand.

"I might nut all in you," he said, licking the gleaming vaginal juices from his lips. "Might make you my next baby mama."

"Do it," Shmoney Rose encouraged. "Cum all in this fat wet pussy. Get me pregnant, big daddy."

As he pounded her out against the door, she couldn't help smiling at the knowledge that she had successfully coerced Aqua's man into fucking the living shit out of her in the backseat of her three-hundred-thousand dollar Bentayga while his personal bodyguard stood to watch outside his door. She'd gotten the SUV in a divorce settlement from Chris Stewart, her MLB player husband of seventeen months. She also received a fire engine red Lamborghini Urus, which was now painted hot pink like her Bentley SUV, eight hundred fifty thousand dollars in stocks and bonds, five point two million dollars in cash, and a sprawling 21st floor Los Angeles penthouse worth twenty one point five million, as well as full custody of their two sons and the two year-old French bulldog she'd name Chief Sosa.

Her Bentayga was parked in the yellow lined *Reserved Parking* section of the massive parking lot behind the twelve-million-dollar gentleman's club. Day-Day entourage had disappeared into the dark colored Mercedes-Benz Sprinter van that was idling behind Shmoney Rose's luxury SUV. Aside from them and the bodyguard, there were just a few others walking to and from their vehicles. Everyone else was inside where all the action was taking place. It was almost eleven o'clock at night. MBM's YoungNya, Bulletface, and Big30 were on the main stage performing the *Step So Hard* remix; while BunnyXXX and Kimmy Kakes moved seductively around the pole, bouncing their surgically enlarged asses for dollars.

Three minutes of steady penetration was all it took for Shmoney Rose to holler out an orgasm and cream all over Day-Day's relentlessly thrusting erection. He leaned down over her suckling at her right breast and slamming his dick in and out of her in a sex-crazed blur and soon Shmoney Rose was experiencing a second jaw-dropping orgasm.

"I'm coming agaaaain," she said in a wavering tone of climatic joy.

"I'm right there with you." Day-Day was really pounding her out now, shoving her legs back and going in as deeply as he could possibly go, his black Pyramid jogging pants and Skims boxer briefs puddled around his Balenciaga sneakers.

He made a growling sound in the back of his throat, and Shmoney Rose felt his dick shudder inside of her. Looking down at his fat brown phallus, she watched it twitch and contract as he ejaculated without ever pulling out of her. Shmoney Rose was a fiend for cum. The thicker the load, the better and she couldn't help dipping two fingers into her gaping hole as soon as he pulled out of her. She brought her semen coated fingers up to her mouth and sucked off all the juices.

"Damn. I love you already," Day-Day said breathlessly as he smiled down at her, stroking the last few drops of semen out of his dick. He moved forward to let Shmoney Rose catch the dangling strand of slime on her tongue, and his smile widened when she took his entire length down her throat and dragged her lips all the way back to the head, slurping him clean.

"Aw, man. See, that's the kinda shit I love, baby. Eat this whole dick. Aqua ain't never done no shit like that."

Shymoney Rose showed a smile of her own; a smile that left her pretty face in an instant when she glanced out her front windshield and saw the two gorgeous women who'd just walked out of the club's rear exit door and stopped right in front of her Bentayga. The two women were Princess and Aqua, and neither of them looked happy to see Davion Carroll on top of her.

Chapter 6

"This bitch is fuckin' my man," Aqua muttered in fluctuating tones of disbelief.

Princess looked over at her dear friend just as a single teardrop went sliding down her unblemished mulatto cheek. As Day-Day's bodyguard turned his attention to them, Princess glanced back at the four bouncers Weezy had entrusted with the task of escorting dancers to their vehicles at the end of their shifts. They were still standing in the doorway, which opened into the wide hallway with an entrance to the health and fitness spa on one side and the tip-out room on the other. Bee Kay and Johnny were holding Princess and Aqua's cash filled black duffel bags, while the other two bouncers walked behind them with pistols holstered on their hips.

"Can I help you?" Day-Day's bodyguard asked.

He was an enormous Samoan-looking man with a mohawk and huge arms that strained against the fabric of his expensive black business suit. His large hands were sheathed in black leather gloves. A plain black skull cap was pulled down over his ears. The frigid winter temperature had turned his nose from brown to red, and his eyes were just as cold.

Princess had been forced to leave the club an hour early. Her half-sister Kamari had a flight to catch at midnight, and Princess didn't have another babysitter. Aqua hadn't felt comfortable leaving the club alone ever since the night a group of masked men in a stolen SUV blocked her off in traffic and robbed her of over five thousand dollars cash and a diamond Cartier watch, so she was leaving out with Princess like she did every night.

Day-Day's bodyguard moved toward the front of the pink Bentayga, on the driver's side, while Aqua headed around to the passenger's side.

"Don't touch my friend," Princess warned.

She was draped in a gray leather Versace trench coat that had set her back over twenty grand, and she had a subcompact .357 Glock 33 in her matching handbag. She reached down into the handbag and closed her fingers around the butt of her pistol, glaring daggers at the giant Samoan. The big man rushed around the rear passenger's side door, reaching it a half second after Aqua and wedging himself between her and the door as Shmoney Rose spun around to engage the lock.

"Get out the truck, you ol' scary-ass bitch!" Aqua shouted.

Her shout brought all of Day-Day's friends out of the idling Sprinter van. Princess went over and pulled Aqua back before the bodyguard could make the fatal mistake of laying his hands on either of them. Day-Day slipped out of the Bentayga's rear driver's side door and hurried over to the Sprinter with his boys, pulling on his shirt and hoodie as he went laughing at the sheer insanity of the moment.

"Girl, fuck that bitch and that nigga. Y'all broke up anyway," Princess said, dragging Aqua along behind her as she stomped off toward her Mercedes.

Aqua didn't put up much of a fight. She'd never been a fighter. Princess had grown up with the Black P. Stones in Hyde Park, at a time when the gang on her block was at war with a neighboring set of Black Disciples; to her, fistfights and shootouts were about as normal as snowball fights.

"I hate that hoe!" Aqua shrieked, her quivering voice replete with emotion. "I don't even want to be on Prime Shift anymore because if I have to spend one second around that rotten pussy having ass bitch, I'll be calling you to bond me out of Cook County Jail."

Princess said nothing. She popped the trunk of her matte black Mercedes-Benz E350 and let the bouncers place her and Aqua's four duffle bags side by side inside it while Aqua fell back against the passenger's side of the Benz and sobbed with her face buried in her hands. Seeing her close friend in distress made Princess want to whip out her Glock and empty its 16-round magazine in the fleeing Sprinter van. Afterall, it was ultimately Day-Day who'd betrayed Aqua, not Shmoney Rose, but she reminded herself that there were cameras everywhere, and also that she and Aqua had well over a hundred thousand dollars in cash in their designer duffel bags.

Johnny helped Aqua into the passenger's seat while Princess got in behind the wheel. She started the engine, took four fifty dollar bills out of her purse and handed them to the bouncers. She set her pistol on her lap and reversed out of the parking space, glowering at Shmoney Rose's pink SUV.

"He wanted me back," Aqua cried. "He said he wanted me back."

Princess ran her hand up and down the back of Aqua's brown mink Louis Vuitton coat. "Don't cry over that man," she whispered consolingly. "He ain't worth it. If he's disrespectful enough to do some bogus shit like that, he never loved you in the first place."

She checked her titanium iPhone 15 Pro. Her boyfriend, Grind's mother had texted her.

Grind said to answer your phone at 8:00 a.m. He'll be calling for a three-way with the lawyer.

She sighed and connected her phone to the charger. She'd only been dating Grind for eighteen days, and already he'd landed himself in the county jail on two counts of attempted murder and one count of fleeing and eluding capture. He was a Ganster Disciple from 69th and Lowe, one of the only GDs to ever come from the predominantly Black Disciple neighborhood. Since meeting him three weeks prior, Princess had invested in him twice, first giving him the twenty-five thousand dollars he'd needed to restock his inventory of fentanyl-laced Percocet, and then when two members of the Hobos street gang tried robbing him at gunpoint on 70th and Emerald and ended stretched out on the sidewalk with multiple gunshot wounds to their upper bodies, Princess had doled out another fifteen thousand to an attorney from the prestigious Bostic & Staples Law Firm.

She texted her sister, Kamari and told her she was on her way home, then refocused on the road ahead as she accelerated out of the parking lot and into the intersection of 73rd Street and Cottage Grove Avenue.

"It's all my fault," Aqua said, whimpering against her door. "I was too busy entertaining other niggas. Lost the good man I had at home. Biggest mistake of my fucking life."

"Nuh uh, bitch. I'm not about to sit and listen to you blaming yourself for his fuckups. He was messaging just as many women, and you're a whole dummy if you let him tell you anything different. He just signed a three-year contract for $105 million. Every bad bitch with even a shred of common sense is in his DM right now. If he really wanted you back, he'd have been all over you, in the backseat of this Benz, not fucking Shmoney Rose in the backseat of her truck. Day-Day started acting shady as soon as he moved to Houston, and you know it."

It was true. When Davion Carroll was traded from the Milwaukee Bucks to the Dallas Mavericks last season, he'd leased a forty-million-dollar Houston mega mansion and moved into it without ever asking Aqua to move in with him. He'd flown her down to see him a few times a week, paid for her second BBL surgery, bought her a 2024 Lincoln Navigator, and padded her bank account with a few hundred grand, but after a month or so he'd broken bad. FaceTime calls became less frequent, arguments became more common, and then, during a shopping trip to Dubai, he'd gone through Aqua's phone while she was dozing on his private jet and found exactly what he was looking for. Indisputable proof that Aqua had been engaging in sexually explicit conversations with several other men, including one of his former teammates. He'd ended things with Aqua the instant the wheels of his Gulfstream G650 touched down on the tarmac at Dubai International, and not even an hour later she'd boarded a Delta flight back to the states with bloodshot eyes and a heavy heart.

Princess had allowed Aqua to cry on her shoulders for a half hour when she got home that night, but she wasn't going for it this time. She had something heavier to ponder that had nothing to do with her emotionally distraught friend or her incarcerated lover, a troubling thought that was eating at her nerves like a school of flesh starved piranhas. Weezy had a trick up his sleeve, and sooner than later, Princess was going to find out what it was.

Chapter 7

The situation between Weezy and Herb began with a phone call from Claudine Whitmore-Sullivan, the woman Weezy had married in 2008 and divorced in July of 2022.

"This man just hit me in front of the kids," Claudine had told him, and that was all Weezy could remember of that particular phone call. His mind had gone blank after hearing of the assault on the love of his life. He and Claudine had always been toxic together, and he put his hands on her a time or three over the course of their fourteen-year relationship, but never had he considered that another would be bold enough to do it. After all, Weezy had a wickedly violent reputation that had followed him from Englewood, where he was born and raised to the Bottom Side neighborhood in the west side of Gary, Indiana, where he and his mother had lived when he and Claudine first crossed paths. He'd done four years in the Indiana Prison System for breaking Claudine's nose in a domestic dispute and then shooting her older brother in the neck, and during his incarceration he'd filed an Eighth Amendment excessive force lawsuit that won him seven point two million. He used the money to invest in Bitcoin right when the cryptocurrency was taking off, and then, when his investment peaked at ninety-eight point seven million, he purchased the spot of land on 73rd and Cottage Grove to build his dream strip club from the ground up.

In the divorce settlement, he'd given Claudine a three-million-dollar Evanston mansion, full custody of their five children, and even twenty-one million, as well as a guaranteed seventy-three thousand per month child support. He signed off on all the papers and watched her leave the courtroom with her new boyfriend, Odell Haggerty in tow. Three days later, she had made that life-changing phone call to Weezy, and he'd shown up outside her boyfriend's Roseland residence in a 1986 Oldsmobile Cutlass Supreme he'd paid a crackhead a hundred dollars to use. He'd been in such a rage that he hadn't even thought to bring a mask. He simply waited with his seat back and a Kalashnikov AK-47 with a 70-round drum magazine attached to its underside, and as soon as the royal blue Mercedes SL 63 Roadster pulled to the curb two car lengths ahead of him, Weezy got out of the rusted old Cutlass and walked up along the driver's side of the AMG convertible with his assault rifle raised and aimed. He'd looked the dark hued younger man in the eyes before he shot him.

Odell "Oats" Haggerty had looked a lot like Weezy in that he was black, heavyset, and cantankerous. Ogrish like Weezy had looked when he first met Claudine; only Weezy was a well-respected gangster who could go just about anywhere in the city, while Oats had claimed to be a Mickey Cobra and was rumored to have cooperated with federal agents to take down a high-ranking GD named Savane Armstrong.

Three pulls of the trigger had sent a trio of 7.62-millimeter rounds through Odell's head and neck, lighting up the night sky in front of the two-story brownstone home and sending a stray black cat diving through the wrought-iron fence. Walking back to his dope fiend rental, Weezy took the time to look around at the other houses, studying the young black couple who went hurrying into a gangway near the corner, and the older man who'd had his dark-colored

90's model Chevy Caprice hiked up on a jack, changing the tire.

"Let another muthafucka hit on my wife," Weezy had shouted in his great, billowing voice. "On folks n'em, they gon' get the same treatment."

No one said a word when he pulled off in the rust-laden Cutlass, and when word from Haggerty family reached Chicago Police Department that he may have had a hand in Odell's murder, he lawyered up and sealed his lips. All that had taken place a year and five months ago. Weezy had practically forgotten all about Odell Haggerty. He'd put all his energy into Queen Of Diamonds. Claudine and the kids had moved into an oceanfront villa in Malibu, California, and since then life had been rather sweet. Then just over forty-eight hours ago, he received a text message from (773)555-0389. *I have video of what happened to Oats. I want ten million, or it goes to the CPD.*" Just below the text was the sixteen second video. It was filmed from a cozy, white-walled upstairs bedroom halfway down the block. Three seconds into the video, the camera zoomed in on the Cutlass's threadbare ragtop, and a young black female had whispered, "That man got a big stupid ass military gun on his lap, and I ain't never seen this car over here before. I bet money he about to shoot somebody."

Odell's AMG entered the frame half a second later, and the girl could be heard whispering, "Ooouu, and that's Oats pullin' up in his drop Benz. He just got with that millionaire bitch from Gary. She bought him that car, paid off that house. He got it made in the shade. Wish I could find me a…"

The girl gasped and went dead silent when Weezy climbed out of the Cutlass with his assault rifle cradled against the belly of his black Givenchy hoodie, the shoulder length dreads he'd had at the time hanging down around his head. He hadn't bothered to pull the hood over his head until after he'd splattered the contents of Odell's skull all over the Roadster's rich leather headrest, and by then the girl who recorded the video zoomed in on his face, and on the diamond-encrusted six-pointed star he'd worn on his thick Cuban-link necklace.

"That's Weezy G!" The girl said with a sharp intake of breath, and then the video ended.

The elderly man, who either foolishly or boldly identified himself as Herbert Harris of Berwyn, Illinois had FaceTimed Weezy from the same mystery number the following afternoon, just as Weezy and a twelve man security team were leaving out of PNC bank at 87th and Cottage with twenty oversized Gucci duffle bags, each stuffed full of cash.

"I see you follow orders," the old man had said, smiling with teeth that were old and stained yellow from decades upon decades of tobacco and coffee abuse. His voice was raspy, and he'd worn a brown, narrow-brimmed top hat that made him look even older than his eighty years. "You just hold on to that bread. I'll take what I need and tell you what to do with the rest. Got a mission for you too. You gon' need to hire some help, and I know just who to ask. I'ma need you to switch Aqua and Princess over to Prime Shift, ya hear me? Gon' need you to do that immediately. Get 'em some chains with the little names on 'em like you do all the other Prime Girls. Give 'em a lil paper to play with, enough to make 'em feel like they owe you. A partner of mine got smoked by one of the Lords a few months back. I need Aqua and Princess to set the pick. You get 'em to do that, I'll cut you a deal. You don't, my boy Big Spicy at Lawrence Correctional Center say he'll pay top dollar if I can get you in a cell with him, and trust me, Big Spicy's a hell of a lot more vicious than Bubba."

Now, as Weezy moved across the main floor inside Queen of Diamonds, socializing with patrons, posing for selfies, critiquing dancers and bartenders on their customer service, the unnervingly malevolent cackle Herb had released before ending the video call kept replaying in his head.

Keck, Keck, Keck, Keck. That was the laugh. The mere memory of that godawful noise made Weezy's blood boil. Snake, Lil D, and Rose G, the three fellow Ganster Disciples who were rarely ever absent from Weezy's circle, stayed a couple of feet behind him as he swaggered through the strip club in his elegant three-piece suit with a tall stack of one dollar bills in one hand. He threw a bunch of them at Bunny XXX as he passed the stage; she beamed in a humble appreciation and bounced her big bubble butt even harder, shifting her attention back to the short light-skinned man who was also showering her in singles.

There were hundreds mixed with the ones that littered the stage floor beneath Bunny XXX and Kimmy Kakes. Legendary gangster rap star, Bulletface had thrown a hundred grand at the two incredibly beautiful young redbones, while YoungNya, his diminutive, little female emcee had thrown a light twenty. Weezy made a mental note to alert Big Gabby as soon as he saw her. There was no better way to humble a sexy ass exotic dancer than to fine her five hundred to a thousand for the most frivolous infraction in the rule book. Especially on a night when the dancer had raked in more cash in four or five hours than most Americans made in an entire year.

Following a hasty visit upstairs to check the very important people in the VIP lounge, Weezy descended the steps in a hurry and was moving toward the elevators in hopes of making a swift return to his office when Big Gabby seemed to appear out of thin air.

"The boys over there by the bar," Big Gabby said, holding her vast hips. "They're from Indianapolis. Princess was talking to the skinny one in the red joggers. The one with the diamond teeth and long dreads. She took him up to one of the blue rooms for two songs, and then she gave him her phone number. They're supposed to be going on a date."

Weezy nodded and shot a brief glance at the tables near the bar. He immediately knew who they were. Stikks and

Fatty were Indianapolis rap artists who always visited QOD when they were in town. Freddie Gibbs was another Indianapolis rapper who loved visiting the club. Weezy had done time with a few of their OG's, so they always came through to show love. The slender young man in the red joggers was a new face, but he seemed comfortable, as if the great city of Chicago were his second home. Cherish Taylor was bent forward in front of him with her back arched and her hands on her knees, rapidly bouncing her bountiful butt cheeks while the young brown hued man laughed and talked with his boys and tossed out forty or fifty dollars at a time.

"Have Cherish meet me in my office as soon as she's done with them," Weezy said to Big Gabby as she stood beside him, scanning the room. He turned to his *"Folks."* Smoke, a lanky, fair-skinned drug hustler with lengthy cornrowed braids, a heavy black Gucci jacket, and a .40 caliber Glock 23 locked and loaded under his matching Gucci sweater; Lil D, Smoke's much shorter, slightly heavier younger brother, and Rose G, an athletically built darker hued GD who'd functioned as an enforcer during his own nine-year prison stint. Weezy gave them a look and motioned for them to follow him to the elevators, and when they were out of everyone else's earshot, he said, "Ay, hit up Freddie and Mike G. Tell them niggas I need 'em to slide through Berwyn, Illinois. I got and address on this old man. If he's there, have lil folks n'em take his top off. All headshots. I got a million dollars cash for whoever gets it done."

Lil D's eyelids flew apart. Stepping onto the elevator with the others, he produced a burner phone from the right-hand pocket of his white and blue Versace sweatpants. He began typing out a message to Mike G, but quickly thought better of it and replaced the smartphone. The doors slid shut before them, and Lil D said, "Fuck that, G. I'll do that shit myself for a million."

"Straight up," Smoke said with a serious chuckle. "On fo'nem grave, we'll get on his ass tonight. Shoot us that address."

Nodding his fat round head and wearing the perpetual scowl that had long ago become his trademark expression, Weezy brought out his own iPhone and went to the notes. He read Herbert Harris's Berwyn, Illinois address out loud. His girlfriend Mikayla Franklin, the thickly proportioned stripper and Only Fans model he'd recently started dating, had obtained the address from her sister Tyesha, who worked as a full-time desk clerk at the Bureau of Motor Vehicles. Tyesha had gladly and gratefully accepted Weezy's twenty thousand dollar cash bribe for the information.

Despite the financial losses he'd suffered in his divorce from Claudine, Weezy still had plenty of dough. He'd only invested seven point three million into the whole Queen of Diamonds project, and he'd already made three million of that back. His PNC bank checking account balance had yet to dip below sixty million and he scraped up another four million in the trenches, purchasing kilos of cocaine, heroin, and crystal meth wholesale from his Arizona supplier and having his underlings distribute them to the dealers in his south side neighborhood. Weezy had money to blow, and like most rich gang members, he didn't mind dispensing a money bag every now and then to take an enemy off the chess board of life.

Weezy stared into the eyes of his fellow Ganster Disciples and smiled at the insatiable hunger he discerned in them. He knew they'd be eager to carry out the murder. Especially for a million-dollar payday. They'd killed for a lot less.

"Yeah, old school," Weezy said, speaking as if Herb was right there in the elevator with them. "You tried to extort a real-life gangster. We gon' show the whole city what that'll getchoo."

Chapter 8

Princess and her sister, Kamari, had gone half on the twenty- two thousand square foot Victorian style mansion that was the centerpiece of Prospect Avenue in Highland Park's coveted *"Millionaires Row"* neighborhood. The house had hit the market at $4.4 million, and the two savvy young businesswomen had snatched it up with an eight hundred thousand dollar cash down payment.

Kamari's deceased father, Lejon "Grizzy" White had married MBM rapper YoungNya. Shortly after, he was shot and killed somewhere on Chicago's west side. He'd left Nya with almost twenty million in their joint bank account. Seeing as YoungNya was currently one of the hottest new female rappers in the music industry, Nya wasn't particularly stingy with the millions she'd inherited from Grizzy. She'd already given Kamari close to nine hundred thousand dollars in drug money. Grizzy had saved up before his untimely death. She'd wired an additional two million dollars to Kamari's checking account, and she'd also transferred two million to Kamari's grandmother, Ne-Ne. Grizzy had wired his mother that very same amount shortly before his passing, so the four hundred thousand Kamari had paid out of her own bank account hadn't affected her as much as Princess's half on the down payment had affected her.

Princess wasn't fortunate to have a millionaire for a father. She was self-made. Every dollar in her bank account was a direct result of her own hard work. Months and months of spinning around poles and dancing on laps. Sure, she had a couple of wealthy men who splurged heavily on her every now and then, but that took work too. She'd given her body and time to those insanely rich creeps for the few hundred grand they kicked her way.

She cruised into her long cobblestone driveway and pulled into the carport next to the enormous house. She got out and helped Aqua lift her duffle bags out of the trunk. They walked alongside each other, past Kamari's blacked-out 2024 Bentley Continental GTC-S to Aqua's off-white Navigator. Princess hugged Aqua goodbye.

"Call me when you get home," she said, silencing the phone alert she'd set to remind her that *Renaissance: A film by Beyonce* would be released in theaters nationwide at the stroke of midnight. "And don't be up all night cryin' over that man. We got plans tomorrow."

Aqua sniffled and nodded her head. She used a napkin to dry her face in the visor mirror. In her skin-tight black leather Louis Vuitton pants and tan colored calf-high boots by the same high-end designer, she was a vision of breathtaking beauty. She started the engine, cut on some Megan Thee Stallion, and drove off without another word, circling the bronze statue in the middle of the vast circular driveway and then accelerating through the open wrought-iron gates.

Princess used the Panneton Home Security app on her phone to close the gates. The phone buzzed in her hand as she walked back to her Mercedes to lift out her own three duffles. It was a text message from Big Gabby: *"No one gave you permission to leave. You and Aqua are fined $1,000 each for leaving an hour early and failing to complete your shifts, so bring $1,050 apiece for tip-ins."*

Gritting her teeth and rolling her eyes, Princess snatched her duffle bags out of the trunk and slammed it shut.

"Fat ass bitch," she muttered as she stormed off toward her side door just as her younger half-sister pulled it open for her.

"You have a good night on that pole?" Kamari asked with a simpering little smirk.

Kamari was twenty, six feet tall, coal-black and drop dead gorgeous. She had natural curves that were even more captivating than the ones Dr. Miami had charged Princess ten grand to mold out of her own gut fat. Kamari was dressed for the cold in a thick blue scarf with a matching fur hat and full-length coat over high-heeled croc-skin boots. All Versace. The coat alone was worth ninety grand.

"I have a good night every night." Princess entered the spacious first-floor kitchen, dropped her duffles on the *Welcome to the BeyHive* rug, and gently kicked the door shut behind her. "It's a mindset. All kinds of strange shit just went down at that shady ass strip club, but I'm not about to let it steal one ounce of my joy. Beyonce's film just dropped, and I'm going to see it first thing tomorrow."

Kamari did a quick little ratchet dance and sang out a Beyonce tune, and then she too was gone. According to the text she'd sent Princess a few minutes ago, she was traveling back to Atlanta on MBM's private jet. YoungNya was pregnant with Grizzy's baby, and her crew of girlfriends, the famous Plus Gang clique, were throwing her a surprise baby shower in the morning.

Princess waved goodbye and shut the door, carried the duffle bags to her bedroom and set them on the floor near the foot of her king-sized Stearns & Foster adjustable bed. She spent a long, silent moment studying her sleeping four-year-old daughter, Vonzella, and wishing the little girl's father wasn't serving out a twelve-year prison sentence for dealing cocaine to a confidential informant. Vonzella, who was called Vee by everyone in the family, had her father's lighter brown complexion. Her hair was in braids with cute little Minnie Mouse barrettes clipped to the ends. She was drooling on her mother's silk encased pillow, lying on her side with the silver Chanel blanket pulled up to her chin. Her favorite toy, Issa Rae's Barbie doll, was clenched firmly in her tiny fist.

Princess snapped a photo of her sleeping angel and then, with an audible sigh, she crossed the room to her spacious walk-in closet. She went in fully clothed and came out seconds later wearing nothing but a fuchsia-colored Givenchy bathrobe. She went into the adjoining bathroom, got the hot water going in her glass doored walk-in shower, and relaxed beneath the cleansing spray, scrubbing her dark brown skin with Dove body wash, soaping and rinsing and lathering up again.

Her calculating mind wandered to Weezy and the fifty thousand he'd given her. There could be something to it, she decided, but she could be overthinking it, as she was prone to do whenever someone offered her something out of the kindness of their heart. She couldn't remember ever getting something for nothing from anybody. There was always a catch, a motive, or as her baby daddy Vonzale was fond of saying, *"The underlay for the overplay."* She sighed and shook her head, forcing herself to think about something else entirely. She snapped a couple of wet nudes for the collection of intimate photos she sometimes sent to the men in her life, and that got her to thinking about Small Body. As if their inner thoughts were somehow linked, Princess's phone buzzed with a new text message from him: *"So when we going on that date??"*

The question brought an ingratiating smile to Princess's comely round visage. She dried off, moisturized, and slipped back into her robe before replying to the text,

"Beyonce's film just came out. I'm going to see that FIRST thing in the morning. We can meet for lunch at one. 86 Prospect Avenue, Highland Park."

She sent the message and returned to her walk-in closet, burning with anticipation as she remembered the slender man's handsome diamond teeth smile, and the alluring scent of his cologne, and the foot-long length of dick he toted in his underwear. She was eyeing her shelved wall of high-end designer heels and handbags, trying to force the sexually explicit thoughts out of her mind and focus on selecting a silver themed outfit for the Queen's concert film debut, when Body texted her again.

"I'll be there."

The ingratiating smile became an elated one. Princess went to the large oval mirror that stood upright between the shelves on the back wall. She posed and snapped another series of provocative photos, keeping her goodies out of sight this time, but leaving just enough cleavage and thigh to give her legion of 986,500 Instagram followers a reason to click on the OnlyFans link in her bio when she posted the pic.

She had a bunch of famous followers. Multimillionaire athletes and actors, Grammy-nominated rap artists and R&B singers, wealthy business owners and moguls of every country and race. Of course there were hundreds of thousands of regular shmegulars, nine-to-fivers who didn't make nearly enough to take care of a woman like Princess, but she never gave them more than a glance. Even Grind had known to come at her with his A-game, purchasing four of her thirty-seven designer handbags the weekend after sliding into her direct messages. Zykarius Lipsey, who played for the Milwaukee Bucks as a small forward and was another one of Davion Carroll's former teammates, had brought all seven of her Hermes Birkin bags, seven designer furs, and seven pairs of seven-inch designer stiletto heels. He'd also transferred exactly $777,777.77 to her Chase bank checking account on their seven-week anniversary. He was a 6'8" bronze skinned athlete who signed a contract that guaranteed him thirty eight million every year for the next three years, and apparently he was superstitious of the number seven. He believed it connected him with God because G was the seventh letter of the alphabet. He always made 7:00 p.m. sex appointments with Princess whenever the Bucks were in town to play the Bulls. Princess didn't mind the numeric obsession. As long as it meant more numbers and commas in her bank account, she didn't mind at all.

She posted one of the mirror selfies and watched the likes pile up until they surpassed ten thousand. It took less than twenty seconds. She set down her phone and selected a silver pair of spiked Christian Louboutin heels and the futuristic silver armored Balmain bodysuit that was an exact replica of the one Queen Bey had worn on the twenty-seventh of June. A silverish-gray Birkin bag completed the look. After laying out her outfit and snapping a photo of it to send Aqua, Princess reached up on tiptoe and pulled down a lambskin Chanel handbag from the top shelf. She'd dropped her new necklace in it before showering, but now she put it back on to model in front of her mirror. She snapped another selfie, this time one purposefully displaying the Cuban-link and name pendant, and when she uploaded it to Instagram, she captioned it with a single diamond emoji.

"Nothing ass bitches," she mumbled, watching the comments accumulate beneath her blinging photos as the vivid memory of Day-Day on top of Shmoney Rose in the back of that pink Bentley truck flashed before her mind's eye. "Let one of you triflin' hoes try and do me like that. I'm bussin' somebody's head over my man. Ex or not."

She sat at her makeup table and removed the Fenty Beauty cosmetics from her face, then tucked the necklace back in her Chanel bag, where *"Big Boy"*, her trusty nine inch dildo, lay hidden beneath a layer of hair extensions and put it back on the top shelf before joining her daughter in bed. Her phone buzzed with a final text message just as she was preparing to shut it off to charge for the night.

"I just googled the address you texted me," Small Body typed. *"I didn't see a restaurant. Looks like a mansion to me."*

Smiling sleepily, Princess replied: *"It's a mansion. And I have a personal chef. Send a list of your favorite foods, whatever you're in the mood to eat, and I'll have it ready for us to eat. See you at the table."* Princess added a smorgasbord of food emojis, shut down the phone, and snuggled up next to her baby girl. She entered dreamland with a content smile on her face.

Chapter 9

Weezy capitalized off his seventy-million-dollar net worth in a variety of ways, one of which was to make sure he was awaken at 10:00 a.m. every morning in a very particular way: to the ominous sound of Chicago drill music, and with a bad bitch in designer lingerie kneeling next in his cotton soft grand Vividus bed, slurping his girthy, black erection in and out of her pretty mouth.

Recently it had been Mikayla, a stunning attractive redbone with freckles, a fat ass, and a curly red afro like Ice Spice, but instead of being from the Bronx, Mikayla and her family were from Chicago Heights. Weezy met her in QOD's VIP Lounge two months ago, the night he'd paid Wooski, Lil Moe 6blocka, and Rooga fifty thousand dollars each to do an hour long show. She had entered the VIP Lounge with some small money college hooper and soon as she got up to use the ladies room, Weezy had sent Blaze in behind her with twenty thousand cash and a phone number. An hour later, she'd sat naked on the edge of his office desk, howling with her head back, her thick legs spread wide, and her perky B-cups bouncing erratically while Weezy's condom sheathed meat log skewered her gushy-wet center. A two hundred thousand dollar shopping spree on *"The Magnificent Mile"* stretch of Michigan Avenue had ensued, and Mikayla hadn't left his side ever since.

This morning, the first of December 2023, Weezy's alarm was Rooga and Lil Moe 6blocka's *Scrappers*, and Mikayla must have been sucking on him for at least the last five minutes or so, because Weezy could feel the subtle tingle in his scrotum, signaling an imminent eruption. He reached to the bedside table to remove his iPhone from the charging cord and check his notifications, his sleep-crusted eyes flicking from the bubbly saliva and wet set of lips that were sliding up and down his dick to the screen on his phone. He had three new text messages. The first one he read was from Newsome "Smoke" Carter: *"Folks, the package ain't at that address. We knocked and everything. No answer, no lights on, nothing."*

The second text was sent three hours later, at 4:17 a.m., and it too was from Smoke: *"Going to the crib to get some Z's. Got Freddie and Mike G on shift at that address, watching for the package. I'll getatchoo when I hear something."*

It was the third text message that made Weezy clench his teeth and flex his nostrils. The old man Herb sent a video. It showed Freddie sitting in a dark-colored Chevy Malibu, his eyes focused on the dark windows of the house he'd been ordered to keep watch over. 1915 South Harlem Avenue, Berwyn, Illinois. It was clear from the shakiness of the video and the cigarette smoke snaking upward in front of the camera that Herb's old arthritic hand was holding the phone.

"You gotta do better than that, Weasel," Herb said. "Do you have any idea how much countersurveillance I did in 'Nam? When I was around your age, my battalion was digging trenches in South Vietnam, slaughtering whole villages. I practically orchestrated the My Lai Massacre, and yet here I sit, sixty some odd years later, a Purple Heart recipient military veteran, watching some wannabe gangster stake out my house. As if I'd be dumb enough to lay my head where I knew you'd look."

The old man went into a troubling fit of hacking coughs, but he recovered quickly. Weezy shot a snotty load of cum in Mikayla's mouth and watched her grimace at the acerbic taste as she sucked it all out of him. She leapt from the bed seconds later, scooping up the oversize Versace shoulder bag he'd brought her as her bare feet went pattering across the heated white marble floor of the incredibly spacious primary bedroom in Weezy's twelve-million-dollar Streeterville condo. She crossed the hallway and disappeared into the bathroom. Weezy would have laughed out loud if not for the video that was still playing on his phone screen.

"Call off your wolves, you fucking weasel," Herb said, once the coughing had subsided. "And for this supremely ignorant little misstep, I want a million dollars in hundreds delivered to my front porch by noon today. I'll send someone to get it. If I don't get my money, you might just end up like this flunky of yours."

At that moment, a hooded figure crept from around the rear end of Freddie's dark sedan, crouching low until he was right up on Freddie's door. Then the man rose up, holding a black handgun with a black sound suppressor screwed into its barrel and a drum magazine attached to its underside. The gun fired on fully auto, numerous muted flashes in a matter of two or three seconds, and the old man's sickeningly wet-sounding cough made a brief laughing return.

"Close that casket, baby," Herb said, chuckling with amusement. "A million dollars in Benjamin Franklin's on my doorstep at noon or else…"

The video ended as the mystery shooter was pulling open Freddie's door and shoving his lifeless corpse onto the passenger seat. Weezy was willing to bet that if he were to visit the exact spot where Freddie had lost his life just a few minutes before sunrise, there wouldn't be a single shard of glass on the street. Probably no blood either. Weezy slipped a hand under his pillow and dragged out his .45 caliber Glock, and when he joined Mikayla in the bathroom to brush his teeth and shower, he took the pistol with him.

He left his 9,500 square foot tri-level condo in a dapper gray Armani suit and tie with a matching Gucci trench coat and skullcap, holding a large gray leather Gucci duffle bag by the straps. Mikayla wore a white Valentino bodysuit, knee-high gator boots by Prada, and a long white fur coat. Her fully loaded white diamond Audemars Piguet watch had cost her one hundred fifty thousand dollard. Weezy was not all that fond of wearing diamond jewelry himself, but his one-of-one green sapphire Richard Mille RM56-01 Tourbillion wristwatch was worth three million. The SUV he selected for the day's travels was his matte black Ferrari Paranaque. He'd paid an additional one hundred thousand over the almost four hundred thousand dollar asking price to have the Ferrari bulletproofed, and one hundred grand more for the professional installation of two unique stash boxes. He was a black James Bond, for all intents and purposes. If James Bond was the loyal protégé of infamous Chicago gangster, Larry Hoover.

Smoke and Lil D were clean-shaven, designer suited, and waiting next to Weezy's Ferrari truck with somber expressions on their high yellow faces. Two matte black Mercedes-Benz G-Wagons sat behind the Paranaque with the engines running and the back doors open. On the backseats sat four grimey street niggas in Dior, Prada, Palm Angels Balenciaga, Gucci, ice on their wrists and fingers. Glocks and Micro Dracos concealed in their designer backpacks and in the back of their waistlines. They were the gang members who'd shown Weezy loyalty over the years, and because of it he'd allowed them to be his personal security, an unofficial job that came with tons of financial perks.

"They found Freddie in an alley a few blocks from that old man's house," Lil D said with a bleak shake of the head. "Somebody shot him in the face and then set the car on fire."

Smoke said, "His family don't even know it's him yet. We only know 'cause we saw the car burnin' on Channel Seven news."

Weezy only flared his nostrils, balled his hands into fists, and gritted his teeth. He handed the heavy duffle to Mikayla so she could stow it away in the trunk of his Ferrari. He searched the faces of Smoke and Lil D's backseat passengers for Mike G.

As if reading Weezy's mind, Lil D said, "Mike G snapped when he found out Folks got whacked. He hit the highway on his way back out there to Berwyn and twelve got on him for speedin'. He did the dash. They had to use the spike strips to stop that Corvette. He in the county."

"What's his bond?" Weezy asked, and before anyone could answer he said, "Never mind. Just find out what it is and send somebody to pay that shit. And put some shorties on them hoes I told y'all about. Princess and Aqua. Just follow 'em until I say otherwise."

There were head nods all around. Lil D and Smoke returned to their G-Wagons. Weezy vanished behind the darkly tinted window of his red passenger's side door, while Mikayla took the driver's side. The three black SUV's full of rich gangsters tore out of the underground parking lot and onto Illinois Street, passing buildings where many of Chicago's wealthiest citizens resided in comfort and luxury.

The incredibly capable Parsonage fastback, technically a crossover, though many still referred to it as Ferrari's SUV had loads of useable room, reclining rear seats, and a top speed of one hundred ninety-three miles per hour thanks to the naturally aspirated V-12 with 725 horsepower. With neatly 7.4 inches of ground clearance, four full-size heated leather seats, and independent four wheel steering, it was no wonder everyone called it a sports utility vehicle.

Weezy sat back in his seat and got on his new titanium iPhone 15 Pro. He googled Herbert Harris and on the fifth page of results found a new article dated March 29, 1971. It said Lt. William Calley of the U.S Army was convicted for the murders of twenty-two South Vietnamese at My Lai on March 16, 1968. Calley's two co-defendants, Johnathan Finley and Herbert Harris, were acquitted of all charges, including the shocking allegations that Harris and Finley had murdered seventy-eight South Vietnamese using flamethrowers and hand grenades. The suspects were highlighted in an accompanying black and white photo, and Weezy could clearly make out a much younger Major Herbert T. Harris. The pitch-black man stood to the right of his convicted lieutenant, a sardonic smile lifting one corner of his thick black lips, a cigarette sticking out from the other side of his mouth.

Weezy shut off his phone screen and sat back for a while with his eyes closed, thinking things over. Herb was going to die soon. Weezy was determined to make that happen. Catching up with the ranking military veteran might prove difficult; especially after Herb got his hands on that million dollars in hundred-dollar bills, but Weezy would get it done. Of the many men who'd crossed him in the past, only three were alive and well, and that was only because they'd been fortunate enough to get arrested before Weezy could get an address on them.

Thinking that Princess and Aqua might somehow be the key to locating Herb, Weezy figured it best to keep a close watch on the two of them. He opened his eyes and made a FaceTime call to Cherish Taylor. The impossibly beautiful Brazilian American woman picked up on the second ring. She had her phone set up next to her blue marble bathtub, angled downward at her curvy naked body as she soaked beneath a mountain of bubbles.

"Sorry about not coming up to see you before I left the club last night," Cherish said, blowing a mound of bubbles off the palm of her hand. "I ended up leaving out with those Nap Town niggas. Small Body, Stikks, Fatty, and their whole lil gang. They came out here to cop some weight from

Millionaire Markio's people out west. When Big Gabby texted me about your little situation with Princess and Aqua, I brought them up to Small Body. He said he didn't know Aqua, but he supposed to be meeting with Princess for lunch this afternoon. I peeped the address when he was texting her. It was 86 Prospect Ave, in Highland Park."

Weezy nodded his bald head and glanced out his window before returning his gaze to Cherish's mouth-watering curves. "Thanks, I needed that. Stop by the office when you get in tonight. Got some'n for you."

"So, wait a minute," Cherish said, and now there was a nipple showing through the bubbles, a glorious little brown nugget in the middle of a small round areola. "Do you want me to keep him here or not?"

Weezy's brow came together. "Keep who there?"

"Small Body. He stayed overnight with me. We're in the Royalty Suite at the Costilla Hotel. You know Aqua caught Shmoney fucking her man last night, so I did the same thing to Princess. Rode that dick all morning. Got him in there passed out."

Weezy chuckled gruffly. "Take a picture in the bed with that nigga and post it to IG. She'll see it eventually."

He ended the video call to keep his own dick from growing hard and after a few more seconds of strategic thought, he sent out two text messages. The first text was to Smoke, and it read, *"Just find out Mike G's bond and shoot it to Big Gabby. Gon' have her bond him out."* The second text went to Big Gabby: *"You know Grind from 69th and Lowe? The nigga Princess been fuckin with? I need you to find out his full name so you can go up to the county jail and pay his bond. You can go ahead and bond Mike G out too. Tell them they owe for that bond money."*

After sending the texts, Weezy set his phone on the armrest and rubbed the rough palms of his battle-scarred hands together, like Cash Money's Birdman. He had a plan; the he first step of which was to apply a certain amount of pressure to the two women Herb was so adamant about using for his little mission.

"Starbucks?" Mikayla asked from the driver's seat.

Weezy shook his head. "Nah, I need to be in my office, and I'ma need you to make a quick stop in Berwyn. I got a bag to drop off on somebody's front porch."

"All the money we just packed into that duffel?" Mikayla cut her eyes at the rearview mirror. "Who you trickin' all that off on? Cause I need me some bands too. I been told you I wanted veneers, and you still ain't bought me a Cuban-link necklace like you gave all them other bitches. Don't think I ain't keepin' track of all this shit."

Weezy cracked a smile for the first time today. He picked up his smartphone, accessed his Zelle banking app, and transferred seventy-five thousand dollars into Mikayla's account. It was more than enough for new teeth and a gaudy diamond necklace. She checked her phone at the next red light and let out an excited shriek, and Weezy reclined his seat again, feeling profoundly calmed by the notable weight of the holstered Glock he had under his left arm, and the Micro Draco he had stashed away in the secret compartment beneath his armrest.

"Thank you so much, big daddy," Mikayla said, her voice replete with emotion. As if he hadn't blown close to a quarter million on her already. She was twenty-six, fourteen years younger than her so-called Big Daddy, and she was undoubtedly one of the baddest young hood bitches Weezy had ever dicked down. He was an ass man, and Mikayla was built like Alexus Costilla in the back. Her eyes were lashy and gray, her full pink lips wetly glossed. Weezy liked her more than he liked most women, not only because she was a certified baddie, but also because she knew how to follow instructions, how to be his second set of eyes, and how to keep her mouth shut when gangster conversations were underway.

Secretly though, Weezy had a thing for Princess Kelly. He'd always been more attracted to darker skinned women, African American paragons of beauty like Tika Sumpter and Kelly Rowland. He had plans to make Princess his second girlfriend once the whole thing with Herb was finished, unless he learned that Princess herself was directly involved in Herb's extortion scheme. In that case, she'd be taking a dirt nap right alongside her octogenarian partner in crime.

Chapter 10

Princess Joya Kelly was named after her thirty-nine-year-old mother Joya Kelly, so the sight of the ice-drenched name pendant hanging from the glistening Cuban-link she wore around her neck hit her spirit in a different way. She paired it with the diamond encrusted Cartier watch she gifted herself the morning after a wealthy OnlyFans subscriber wired her two hundred thousand. She'd also bought her brand-new E-Class Mercedes that morning.

She stood staring at the name pendant in her closet mirror, dressed in a green Fendi tube top with matching leggings and Balenciaga sneakers. Then her eyes fell to her sleeping daughter, who had fallen asleep on the plush pink carpet behind her after they returned from seeing Queen Bey's three hour concert film.

The short and long hands on her Cartier watch told Princess it was 12:21 p.m. part of her was upset at Aqua for not joining her and Vee at the theater, but she understood. Aqua was an emotional wreck. She'd stayed up late into the morning on FaceTime with Day-Day, arguing and crying, and shouting expletives, hanging up and calling back and hanging up again. Exposing her relationship woes on Instagram Live as she paced the cherrywood living room floor of her 9,200 square foot Streeterville townhouse. Looking like a rich, spoiled brat to the three point seven million followers she amassed over the years.

As far as Princess was concerned, Aqua could keep her negative vibes in Streeterville. There would be no frowns in Princess's world today. A self-proclaimed member of the Bey Hive, Princess was in the very best of moods, and there was virtually nothing that could bring down her spirit after experiencing the sheer genius of Beyonce on the silver screen.

Princess's personal chef, a chubby brown hued man called E-Rock, and his eight-person team of culinary experts had prepared a feast fit for a princess. She'd paid Mariah Porter of Mariah's Salon five crisp hundreds to stop by and touch up her hair and nails at seven o'clock this morning. Her mom had arrived ten minutes ago to take Vee back to her place in Dayton, Ohio Rogers neighborhood for the weekend. Joya was in Vee's enormous Barbie themed bedroom across the hallway, packing Vee's luggage with clothes, toys and other adolescent necessities.

Princess snapped a couple of sexy mirror selfies and posted them to Instagram before leaving the closet to join her mother in Vee's room. Joya was sitting Indian-style on the floor with Vee's pink Louis Vuitton suitcase laid open before her, a spitting image of the twenty-two-year-old African American sex goddess she'd produced. A devout Black Lives Matter activist, she wore a clingy black Balenciaga jogger over a splashy new pair of black and red Air Jordan 1 sneakers.

"Where are those lavender Uggs I brought Vee for her birthday?" Joya asked, glancing up at Princess. She paused to ogle the new bling and nodded smiling. "Okay. I see you, Prinny Prinn. Iced Out on these bitches. Ouuu and I like that big diamond crown over the P. Adds a unique edge to the piece. I like it."

Princess beamed in appreciation of the compliment and rolled her eyes dramatically. "Those boots are in my closet. Vee likes to switch out of her clothes and shoes to pose in front of the mirror with me."

"Did you get a chance to talk to your sister before she left?"

"For a second. She was already dressed and on her way out the door when I walked in last night." Princess went to Vee's bed and sat down. The bed looked like a pink Barbie jeep with a big square mattress in the middle.

"I still ain't really spoken with her about Grizzy."

Joya shook her head despondently. "Neither have I. Not since the funeral. She starts crying every time I mention her daddy, so I stopped bringing him up."

She rearranged a pile of child-sized designer sweaters in the suitcase to wedge in Vee's iPad.

"She's taking it kinda hard, but I have to admit, all that money Nya gave Kamari is helping her through the grief. Kamari's a millionaire at twenty. And she's always hanging out with all those rap stars. I mean, I know she misses her daddy like crazy, but she's practically the same age as Nya, and they're out partying on yachts and private planes every night. Kamari dropped out of college to model fulltime, and it's paying off more than any career she could've ever dreamed of getting with that degree. She'll be modeling for Ralph Lauren in next month's Vogue."

"I know," Princess said. "She went half on this house with me and barely even lives here."

"It's that Johnna Broward chick," Joya said accusingly. "She's the billionaire CEO of that Panneton Tech home security company, and ever since it came out that she and Grizzy had the same daddy, she's been spoiling Kamari too. She gave Kamari the keys to a thirty-million-dollar Miami penthouse the other day."

Princess's neatly groomed eyebrows went high. Kamari had told her about a wild male stripper party she and more than eighty of her sorority sisters had thrown at some massive oceanfront penthouse two nights ago, but she hadn't known that Kamari's Aunt Johnna actually owned the place. She googled Johnna Broward, and the next two transparent words Google suggested were *net worth*. She clicked on it. As of November 1st, 2023, *Forbes* had Johnna Browards' reported net worth listed at 21.2 billion, edging out Abigail Johnson to take the number seventy-five spot on the list of world's wealthiest individuals. Princess didn't need to click on the actual link to the full Top 100 list to know whose name had the number one spot, but she did it anyway.

#1 Alexus Costilla-King net worth $231 billion. Princess salivated at the mere notion of such wealth. Alexus was a huge source of inspiration to many black and brown women worldwide. She was the stunningly attractive icon who'd crashed through the glass ceiling of insane wealth. Her tall, dark, and well-muscled husband was none other than Blake "Bulletface" King, the Grammy Award winning drill rapper and CEO Of Money Bagz Management whose personal net worth was just shy of $3.8 billion. Since signing Chicago's own Nya Mixon, AKA YoungNya to MBM, Nya had reportedly amassed her own little fortune of $27 million.

"So, who's the man you got coming over for lunch?" Joya asked, snapping Princess out of her wealthy reveries. "I saw that dining table. You could feed a village."

"Find you some business, Mama. Ain't that what you always told me?"

"Mmm hmm." A suggestive smirk lifted one corner of Joya's pretty mouth. "You just make sure he wraps it up. I got enough on my plate with Vee, and I am done changing shitty diapers."

Princess's phone rang in her hand. She looked down at it and knitted her brow when she saw that is was Yasmine "BunnyXXX" Gordon, the Prime Time Girl who was also one of her favorite adult film stars. It was the first communication she'd received from anyone in PTG, and it made sense. Bunny was a genuinely nice person. Having gained notoriety from her viral blowjob videos, she was essentially the new Superhead. There weren't many porn viewers in America who hadn't watched her in action at least once.

Slipping an Airpods Pro in her left ear, Princess answered the call.

"Good afternoon," Bunny said immediately.

"Hey, what's up?" Princess asked in the deadest of tones. She was automatically on edge. After having seen Shmoney Rose folded in half beneath Davion Carroll in the backseat of that hot pink Bentayga, she was instinctively cautious of every member of PTG.

"Okay, first of all, I am not against you," Bunny began. "Just wanted to make that perfectly clear. I honestly don't care who they switch over to Prime Shift. I'm here for the money. I talked with Kimmy Kakes and Sasha the Stallion about it, and Kimmy talked to Thick Doll. We all feel the same way. The only bitches mad is Shmoney Rose and Cherish Taylor. Speaking of which..."

Bunny elongated the word speaking, and Princess knew right away that there was trouble brewing. She got up and went out into the hallway to keep her mother from eavesdropping, and Bunny continued.

"Cherish shared a video to her IG stories. She's in bed with the same scrawny lil brown skinned nigga with the dreads, and apparently it's some kinda shot at you. I just didn't want you getting blindsided by it."

"Hold on a second," Princess said as she pulled up her Instagram app and searched for Cherish Taylor's page. She touched Cherish's profile photo to view the Instagram stories and gritted her teeth when she saw Small Body lying in bed beside Cherish with a blunt burning between his lips. Princess felt the wet splat of her heart landing in the pit of her stomach. She took a deep, calming breath, and nodded her head threateningly.

"I'll call you back," she said, and ended the call before Bunny could say anything more.

Vee must have awakened and recognized the distant fragrance of her grandmother's Chanel No.5 perfume, because at that moment she went darting past her mother's legs with her Issa Rae doll clutched tightly in one fist, out of one bedroom and into the next.

"Grammyyyy!" Vee shrieked.

"Lil girl if you don't get off me," Joya replied laughingly.

Lowering her head and squeezing her eyes shut, Princess muttered, "I'm good. Fuck that bitch. And fuck that nigga too. I only invited him over cause Grind ain't out and I knew Body was from a whole nother city. I'm bogus for tryna cheat on my nigga in the first place."

When she opened her eyes and raised her head, inhaling the scrumptious aroma of the feast her chef and his team had spread out on her eighteen seat dining table, she exited Instagram to view the Panneton home security notification she just received. It was a proximity alert. Someone had just pulled up to the wrought iron gates in front of her house in a black Mercedes G-Wagon that looked a lot like the trucks that were always trailing behind Weezy. Princess zoomed in on the man who climbed out of the front passenger's side door of the Benz truck. She gasped when she saw who it was. His name was Vincent Rose. His nickname was Grind and somehow he'd managed to get himself released from Cook County Jail on a one-million-dollar cash bond.

Chapter 11

This will be BunnyXXX's second gangbang scene, and judging from the intimidating lengths and girths of the huge black penises the four brawny men were eagerly stroking to life in front of her, she was in trouble. After the call with Princess, she dropped her smartphone in her white leather Birkin bag and set it on a nearby end table. She drank a sixteen-ounce bottle of mineral water and did a breathing exercise to clear her mind of all the strip club drama and focus on becoming the brown hued sex goddess the male porn actors expected her to be.

The Lucid Entertainment film production crew were busy plugging in cords and testing their high-definition cameras and microphones. Noble King, not only the CEO of Lucid, but also the director of this particular gangbang, was seated in his director's chair, surrounded by three chattering assistants. He usually dressed the way Weezy dressed, in designer business suits and loafers. Today he donned a more casual attire, a white hoodie with *AMIRI* printed across the chest in dripping black lettering, white sweatpants, and a black and white pair of Amiri sneakers. No dreadlocks for Noble; he was an older black man who knew how to blend in with the lower rungs of society, those who weren't fortunate enough to have a net worth of four hundred and ten million.

Two of the cameras were already focused on Bunny, and for a damn good reason. She was a statuesque, caramel complected twenty-one year old black woman with a 27-inch waistline and 46-inch hips. Her perky 34C tits were as fake as her big bouncy ass, but they looked spectacular on camera and in person too. With her cute pink lips, chinky brown eyes, high cheekbones, and slender figure, she was the epitome of a dime piece.

One production assistant, a short, large breasted white blonde named Whitney Manges came over to remind Bunny of Noble's vision for the scene.

"Okay, so, you'll be wearing a tiny little pair of booty shorts and a belly shirt. This guy here…" Whitney turned to point at Tyrone Steele, a porn legend with a devastatingly lengthy fourteen-inch erection "Is your boyfriend, and the other three men are his friends. They'll be playing some kind of NBA game on that PS5 over there. You'll walk in and stand in front of Steele, he'll reach out to squeeze on your ass and rub your pussy, and then he'll ask you to suck him off in front of his boys. That'll be your cue to kneel down in front of Steele and wrangle out that fat black snake of his, and you can just go to town after that. His boys will eventually stand up to join in. You'll hear the cues through your earpieces."

Bunny nodded her consent. Her pussy was soaking wet, just like it always got when she was ready to have sex, whether on or off camera. Her nipples had hardened as soon as she saw Tyrone's dick out of his sweatpants. He was tall, dark, and baldheaded. Her favorite kind of black man, and his long, black dick stuck straight out in front of him like a frozen python. The forty-five-year-old porn vet and his three "boys" represented just one percent of Lucid's black male roster, but none of them were as famous as Tyrone Steele. Every hot-blooded woman in the adult film world wanted to shoot a scene with Tyrone. This would be Bunny's second scene with him, and the first time she'd actually get to fuck him on camera. Their first scene was the fourth of the seventeen viral blowjob videos she'd uploaded to her

Pornhub page, the one that had been viewed over eleven million times to date. The one that had won her a 2022 AVN Award for "The Best Blowjob of the Year."

The production assistant walked away and returned a minute later to hand Bunny a small, folded pair of navy booty shorts, and equally tiny half of a white shirt with *Cum Slut* airbrushed across the chest in big pink and red cursive lettering, and a tube of KY lubricant. Then she led Bunny out of the massive living room, through a set of French doors, down a redwood floored hallway, and into a huge bathroom with televisions embedded in the walls of the glass-encased marble shower.

"You're gonna need that lube," the blonde said. "Tyrone took one of those pain pills that makes him last forever, and you know he's been wanting to fuck you on camera ever since you made him cum in under three minutes in that fourth Throat Goat video."

Bunny snickered guiltily. The blonde left the bathroom, and Bunny changed out of her white denim jeans and white Chanel sweater. She decided to keep her off-white Dior sneakers on for the shoot. She'd brought her purse with her from the living room. After all, a girl couldn't just leave a one hundred ten thousand dollar Hermes handbag unattended, and her iPhone began to ring as she was fingering her asshole with lube. She took out her smartphone and looked at it. Big Gabby was calling. The same Big Gabby who'd charged her a hundred dollar "late-to-stage" fee eight times in the past month. The same Big Gabby who'd hit her with a one thousand dollar fine for failing to appear on stage altogether the night she tested positive for Covid-19, but the fact remained that Big Gabby was the House Mom at QOD. There was no money like strip club money. As an adult film star, Bunny had made all kinds of money off hosting gigs and private bookings, but the most she'd ever been paid for a porn scene was eighty five hundred dollars. Meanwhile, at QOD, there were nights when she went home with $30,000 to $40,000, and she always cleared at least three of four grand on the worst of nights. She was lucky to do four sex scenes in a month, while the strip club dollars came in every night she felt like twerking as long as she abided by the House Mom's ever-growing list of rules. Bunny answered the call and placed her phone on the rim of the marble sink.

"Hey, Gabbs," she said, trying to sound as kind and good-natured as humanly possible.

"I need your opinion on something," Big Gabby said in a low whisper.

"Sure, what is it?"

Big Gabby hesitated. "You can't speak about this to anybody."

"My lips are sealed."

"Okay, so do you remember me telling you that I had to have that life-saving surgery early last year, and when I didn't have the cash on hand to get it done myself, my Auntie Crystal asked Millionaire Markio, and he gave me his last thirty grand?"

Bunny nodded as if Gabby could see her and said, "Yeah, I remember."

"Well, listen to this…and again, this stays strictly between me and you."

Bunny sighed. "I heard you the first time, Big Gabby."

"Weezy just got in about an hour ago. I went up to his office to go over the stage plan for tonight's special guest performance, but he got a phone call before I could get a word out. It was a call from the old man who's been trying to extort him over that video."

Another furrowing of the brow. "What video?" Bunny asked. She was pulling the skintight booty shorts over her huge round bubble of an ass.

This time it was Big Gabby who let out a sigh. "I can't go into all the specifics. Let's just say this old man has Weezy on camera doing something that could get him a life sentence. But anyway, that old man is the reason Aqua and Princess got moved to the Prime Shift. He wanted them there and we just found out why." She paused for dramatic effect and then sailed on. "The old man wants Aqua and Princess to set up Millionaire Markio."

Bunny looked down at the crotch of her spandex shorts to make sure the plump print of her pussy was visible through the thin fabric, but the whole time her mind was glued to that name she'd just heard.

Millionaire Markio.

She knew him well. She'd had a threesome with him and his famous ex-girlfriend, Nikkia Staples, sucking his dick while Nikkia rode his mouth. Bunny's friend Whitney Clarrett had dated him for over a year before he left her for Nikkia. Soon thereafter, Whitney had been kidnapped from the parking lot of a west side Chicago strip club, and she hadn't been seen or heard from since.

"What did Markio supposedly do to this old man?" Bunny asked.

"He killed somebody. Or at least that's what the old man thinks. I don't know. All I know for sure is that the old man wants Princess and Aqua to set up Markio to be killed, and for some reason he needs them on Prime Shift to make it happen."

Bunny wanted to hear more, but at the very moment another assistant knocked at the bathroom door and shouted at her.

"Five minutes till action. We need to get you oiled up."

"Come on in," Bunny said, and to Big Gabby she whispered, "I gotta go. Got a scene to shoot. I'll call you back when we're finished."

"Is this the scene you were supposed to be doing with Tyrone Steele?" Big Gabby asked with a discernible level of excitement in her tone. "Because if it is, you can tell him to bring that big ol' horse dick over here. Tell him I pay like I weigh, baby."

"Bye, Gabby," Bunny said, laughing.

She ended the call, and while the two college-age female assistants rubbed her down with body oil, one reoccurring question kept popping up in her head. *"What had her boyfriend Markio done to make someone want to kill him?"*

Chapter 12

Big Gabby's mind was in the gutter. Right after the phone call with Bunny, she accessed the Internet on her iPhone, went to Pornhub, and typed in "Tyrone Steele." She strolled through videos until she found one titled Tyrone Steele Slays BBW Monroe Sugars, Huge Cum shot. She got up from her swivel chair and crossed the room to her office door, shut and locked it, and returned to her black leather chair. She glanced at the many camera images on her desktop computer screen. There wasn't much action going on inside Queen of Diamonds at this time of day. Just seven girls on the floor and one on stage, entertaining the small crowd of nine to five office workers who'd come in on their lunch breaks. There were nineteen strippers in training on the third floor, learning how to ride the pole under the tutelage of strip club veteran, Lola Cheeks.

Big Gabby was a big girl. Five feet eleven inches tall, two hundred eighty pounds. Today she donned a lavender Gucci print mini dress over matching Maison Margiela Tabi Mary Janes. Her Prada purse and the highlights in her blond shoulder length wig were lavender in color. She lifted the hem of her dress and parted her meaty brown thighs. She wasn't wearing any panties. Her clitoris was rigid with arousal. She licked two fingers and used them to massage her clit as she pressed play on the video.

It began with Tyrone Steele and Monroe Sugars reclined in the lounge chairs beside a massive backyard swimming pool. Palm trees swayed in the background. Tyrone was shirtless, his bald head and sharply defined abs glistening in the Florida sunshine. There was a notable bulge in the front of his black mesh gym shorts. He had an issue of Chicago Magazine open in his veined black hands, but his eyes were on Monroe Sugars, and her eyes were on him. The scene progressed to Tyrone walking and speaking with Monroe, and seconds later she was tugging down his shorts. His long flaccid dick flipped out like a dead black snake. Big Gabby's mouth watered at the sight of it. As Monroe Sugars closed her hand around the base of Tyrone's dick and sucked the bulbous head into her mouth, Big Gabby stood her phone against her computer monitor, raised and spread her thick thighs apart, and shoved two fingers into her gushy wet pussy hole. She began to finger herself, watching Monroe's succulent red lips sliding along the intimidating length and girth of Tyrone's fat black erection.

"Suck on that dick, girl," Gabby said.

She licked her own lips, trying to imagine the taste of Tyrone's dick on her tongue. The bitter saltiness of skin and precum. The gagging sensation every time the head of his fourteen-inch pole struck her dangling pink tonsils. Shooting another quick glance at her computer, she saw that an old dark-skinned man in a wide brimmed hat had just entered the strip club. He was as black as a native Nigerian, dressed in a black turtleneck sweater and slacks that fit snugly on his rail thin frame. He walked with a black cane in his right hand. The two equally dark hued women who walked in with him appeared to be much younger in age, maybe in their twenties or early thirties, and they wore black pantsuits with black Covid masks over the lower halves of their faces. The three of them went to a table near the front doors, sat down, and summoned the bartender. Big Gabby squinted at the camera image, but only for a couple of seconds. Her gaze quickly returned to the screen of her iPhone, and she let out a low moan as an intense tingle shot through the thousands of nerve endings in her clitoris.

It was the tears in Monroe's lashy dark eyes that elicited the moan. The poor woman was choking on all that meat, forcing it way down the back of her throat as she stared up at Tyrone Steele and massaged his heavily hanging nut sack in one hand. She was sitting up on the lounge chair with her head turned to face him, and his strong black hands were holding the back of her head.

"I'ma nut all in yo' pretty ass face," he said.

He bit down on his bottom lip and thrust his hips forward, fucking her throat. Bubbly white saliva accumulated along the first six or seven inches of his dick.

"Yeah. Just like that. Give me all that throat. I wanna see stretch marks in the back of that throat when I'm done with you."

Monroe Sugars did as he asked and gave him all of her throat. Big Gabby liked the fact that Monroe was a heavy-set girl like her. Monroe was better proportioned and lighter in complexion, but their body types were quite similar. Big Gabby had a few more rolls here and there, and her 58-inch hips were maybe eight or nine inches wider than Monroe's, but they were the same height.

Big Gabby had no worries about being caught in the act of masturbating. She had smoked glass in her office door, and her wall mounted Panneton Office Fortress Pro camera was accessible only from her and Weezy's computers. Weezy had watched her play with her pussy several times over the past couple of months. He said it made his dick hard. It made him want to fuck the brains out of her.

Framed photos of Big Gabby with her favorite club guests hung from the cherrywood walls. There was one of her with Dreezy, a second one with Katie Got Bandz, and a third one with Fendi Da Rapper. Another showed her with an arm wrapped around Millionaire Markio, the bestselling urban fiction novelist who'd paid for her life-saving surgery last summer. Big Gabby favorite photo of all showed her standing with the couple who was arguably the most famous Black couple in America, Blake "Bulletface" King and Alexus Costilla-King. They had a combined net worth of over $230 *billion*. The kind of wealth that could feed a thousand generations of Kings. One supportive TikTok video from Alexus "Queen A" Costilla was all it had taken for Big Gabby's lingerie to sell out online. Right now, though, lingerie sales were the furthest thing from Big Gabby's mind. Tyrone Steele had her full attention, and though she was mildly irritated that Bunny was more than likely blessing Tyrone with her famously sloppy wet fellatio at this very moment, she was still able to focus on her own vivid imagination, fucking herself with two fingers as she watched the porn video in front of her.

Tyrone had just turned Monroe Sugars around and was stretching her butthole open with the head of his dick when Big Gabby tensed up and trembled through a teeth-clenching orgasm that left her juices dripping off the edge of her leather swivel chair. She tidied up in a hurry, using four disposable wet wipes to clean all the creamy vaginal juices from her fingers, her labia, and the seat of her chair, and she didn't even think of the old man again until she happened to cast another glance at her computer monitor a minute or so later. By then Weezy had already left his second floor office and was walking toward the old man's table with a whole lot of pep in his step. The same Weezy who'd butchered a man so severely in prison that the man had lost an eye and was now paralyzed from the waist down. This same Weezy, who just yesterday had cleared exactly $137,841.54 from house fees, fines, and alcohol and ticket sales. The sheer amount of aggression in Weezy's gait caused Big Gabby's eyes to widen in shock and fear, and she knew right away that the old man seated with the two young women was Herbert Harris.

Chapter 13

Weezy's thick nostrils were flared wide, his huge dark hands were balled into huge fists, and his heavy footfalls were like sledgehammer strikes as he approached the table where the old man was seated. He placed his large hands flat on the table and leaned forward, scowling at Herb's wrinkled black face. One of the two women snickered at the palpable animosity.

"Nice place you got here," Herb said in his creaky old voice. He eyed a passing dancer, licked his lips and nodded his head. "Real nice."

The slimmer of the two women snickered again. Her eyes were hidden behind Dior sunglasses. Her fingernails were neatly manicured claws, painted black. Weezy had a sneaking suspicion that she had gotten a decent share of the cash he'd had delivered to Herb's Berwyn home.

"You must think I'm some kind of fuck nigga," Weezy said, his tone low and menacing. Herb stood about six feet even; at 6'9" Weezy towered over him and his two female minions. "I'm a real GD, old man. I'll kill yo' old ass right here, right in front of these two dumb bitches you brought with you.?

"Do I look like I'm worried about you touching me?" Herb asked as if the idea of Weezy passing a serious threat to him was beyond the realm of possibility. "I'm here to talk business. Here to help you out. Thanksgivin' wasn't but a couple of days ago. You should at least have a little thanks left in you."

Weezy looked at Herb and said nothing. He wondered if one of the women seated on either side of the old man was the recorders of the incriminating homicide video. He had Mikayla's sister look into the names and addresses of the other residents on the block, but nothing had come of it. There were four other Black households on the block. Lil D had spotted a teenage girl in an upstairs window halfway down the street, but when he approached her as she walked up the sidewalk to the corner store. He'd recorded her voice, and it hadn't sounded anything like the girl from the video.

"Now," Herb said, cracking a smile. His gums were dark and leathery with age, and his teeth were far too white and perfectly square to be the same mouthful God had given him in the early 1940's.

"Let's get to the business part of this whole thing. Millionaire Markio."

"Talk," Weezy said and that was all.

"He'll be here on the first of February to celebrate his birthday, and he'll have forty or fifty Vice Lords with him, so we can pretty much rule out getting rid of him in the traditional gangster way. They're too heavily armed, with too many soldiers ready and willing to shoot first and ask questions never. But Markio's got a weakness. That rich lawyer chick broke it off with him a few months back. He's single now, and he follows Princess and Aqua on all those social media platforms, comments under their photos all the time. I need them to set him up for the kill, and I want you to pull the trigger. You do that for me, and that video will disappear."

Weezy's eyelids became narrow slits. He leaned in over the table and glared menacingly at the clearly unbothered octogenarian. The two women eased back in their seats, clutching their purses, but Herb didn't move a single inch. There was a viable reason for the searing hot rage that blazed a fiery path through Weezy's veins at that very moment. He and Markio went way back. They had done time together at Indiana State Prison. Markio as a ranking member of the Vice Lords, Weezy as a highly respected and deeply feared enforcer of for the Ganster Disciples. Weezy had done some real slimeball things to the bitch niggas he'd done time around, but Markio was a real nigga who'd gone into prison the same way he'd came out----respected, honored, and certified in the trenches as a stand-up gang member who'd never folded under pressure or cooperated with the authorities. The kind of guy Weezy would never in his life turn his back on. Which is why, in a blinding flash of contempt, Weezy shot his musclebound right arm straight out toward Herb's leathery old neck. His huge hand open, thick brown fingers curled to grab and squeeze, but the Vietnam veteran was much more agile than Weezy anticipated. He dipped back against the plushy upholstered royal blue bench seat, and his cane swung up, over, and down in a viciously fast arc. The gleaming steel 24-inch sword blade that had been concealed inside the cane cut right through the flesh and bone of Weezy's wrist. The hand came off in a spray of blood that left a copious crimson mist spread across Herb's face and neck.

Weezy stumbled rearward, cradling his gushing stump of an arm against his chest just as Big Gabby and two daytime bouncers, Adonis and Fat Perry came rushing up beside him. He gawked in shocking disbelief of the grisly sight of his severed hand as it lay palm up on the smooth tabletop, the fingers twitching so spasmodically that the two diamond rings on the pinkie and middle fingers made a clacking noise against the expensive granite. Big Gabby wrapped her arms around Weezy and screamed like a banshee.

"Oh my God! His hand! His hand! Perry, get his hand!"

Herb rose slowly from the table, extending the sharp, dripping end of his sword toward the bouncers. He licked the blood from his lips and cracked a nefarious grin as he and his two young lady friends backed toward the front doors. Adonis moved to intercept Herb, and one of Herb's women produced a subcompact pistol from inside her shiny black Gucci purse. She aimed it right at Adonis forehead, stopping him in his tracks.

"February first, you hear?" Herb said to Weezy. "Two months from today. You take care of that, and the video disappears."

With that, the old man and his mysterious women were gone.

As Fat Perry and Adonis were tying a belt around Weezy's bleeding stump, Big Gabby raised her phone to dial 9-1-1.

Weezy waved his hand to stop her. "Nah," he said, struggling to maintain control of the situation as the edges of his vison became increasingly blurry. "Get a bucket of ice and stick my hand down in it. Adonis and Perry will get me to a hospital. You go up to my office and delete this camera footage. No police."

Weezy was in and out of consciousness after that. Once second he was being rushed past panic-stricken exotic dancers and open-mouthed club patrons, and the next he was laid out on the backseat of Fat Perry's clean black Tahoe, blinking at the ceiling and rocking from side to side as the SUV went screeching out the parking lot.

"Hold on back there, Weezy," Adonis said. "You gon' be good, folks. The bleeding done slowed down a lot. We'll be at the hospital in three minutes. Who the fuck is that old man?"

"A dead man," Weezy replied. He could feel the hot blood on his chest, matting the silky fabric of his shirt to his skin. "As soon as I get up close to that sneaky old bastard again, he's a dead man."

Chapter 14

"They put me in a cell with a heavy hitter," Grind was saying as he chewed and swallowed a mouthful of spaghetti and lobster. "One of the Folks from Jaro City. He sent his lil brother over there to buy all the rest of them pills from my sister. Paid her the whole forty bands up front. I was just about to call and tell you about it when they buzzed my door and told me I had made bail. Weezy had Big Gabby bond me out."

Princess swiftly looked up from her own plate of steak, mac and cheese, and crab legs. She wiped the stunned expression off her face before Grind could catch sight of it, but her mind remained stuck on his words.

"Weezy," she thought introspectively. *"Now why in the hell would he go and bond my boyfriend out of jail? I know they're both GD's, but they're not friends. They hardly even know each other."* She drew her lips thin and nodded her head thoughtfully.

Her phone vibrated next to her cold glass of orange juice. She checked the notification and saw that it was a text message from Small Body. *"My bad, lil mama. Slept late. Can I still slide on you?"*

She replied. *"Hell to the mfn no. Delete my number please and thank you."*

She blocked him and deleted the text thread. *Good riddance.*

Staring across the table at Grind, Princess couldn't repress the intrigued smirk that began at one corner of her mouth and quickly spread to the other. He was tall, light brown in complexion, and arrogant in a quiet way. He had waves that were usually sharply lined and tapered, but a few weeks without a barber had him looking scraggly about the face. He wore the same dark blue Givenchy jogger he'd worn the day he was arrested and blue and white Air Jordan 4's. It was the outfit he'd purchased during their Mag Mile shopping spree just a few hours before his arrest. He'd already found himself another pistol; a Glock with a 30 shot extended clip lay on the table next to his plate. Princess didn't know how to feel about the gun; especially since, for some unknown reason, Weezy had just dropped a million dollars to get Grind out of jail.

"Wonder what made him bond you out," she pondered aloud.

Grind shrugged. "Fuck me up too. I mean, don't get me wrong, I know Folks from around the way, but I ain't never hung out with him or nothing. He had Lil D give me his number and drop me off over here. I'm supposed to hit him up later tonight."

"Hm. That's odd, don't you think?"

"Shit, I'm happy to be free. I wouldn't give a fuck why he did it. Folks looked out for me. He had Lil D give me this glizzy and put fifty racks in my pocket, and that's on top of the million he put up for me to get out. I owe him for that."

Princess nodded and went on eating. Thinking. Occasionally picking up her phone to stroll through TikTok and Instagram. She had a lot on her mind. Weezy and his questionable actions; Aqua and her relationship dilemma; the scheduling change to Prime Shift and all the drama that was almost certain to come along with it.

After a time, Grind swept his gaze across the table and shook his head in disbelief. "This a whole lot of food for one person," he said, studying the dishes. "Was you expecting company?"

"Mm hmm." Princess lied. "Thought my mama was gon' stay for a while. Didn't expect her to leave so soon."

"You still got that bag I left over here?"

Another nod from Princess. She'd gone through the tan leather backpack twice already. Inside it was a little over sixty thousand dollars in cash, a few hygiene products, a fresh pair of Calvin Klein underwear, and a modified Glock 19 with two extra clips.

"I'ma need those trimmers to get all this hair off my face," Grind said, stroking his incipient sideburns.

"Good. I hate sitting on beards."

Grind chuckled. "You know you got me fucked up, right?" He got up, wiping his mouth with a napkin. "Meet me in that bedroom in about twenty minutes. I got some'n for yo' shit talkin' ass."

Princess smirk widened into a full-on smile, She couldn't wait.

Chapter 15

Thirty-year old Vincent "Grind" Rose stood naked in front of the rarely used bathroom that he always used when he came to Princess's palatial home, trimming down the hairs on his face and around his groin while he thought over everything Lil D had told him during the brief ride from Cook County Jail to Highland Park.

"Weezy fanned a nigga down some months back," Lil D had said. "He ain't know somebody was recordin' the whole shit until a few days ago, when this old man named Herb contacted him on some extortion type shit. Sent Folks the video and demanded ten million to make it go away.

"Damn," Grind had replied.

"That ain't the half of it. We found out where the old maid laid his head and sent one of the folks over there to catch him leavin' out and nail his old ass, but the old nigga was two steps ahead of us. He called Weezy on Facetime and had somebody shoot Freddie all in the face right there on video, so Weezy could see it. Threatened to send the video of Weezy blowin' ole boy down to the law if Weezy didn't bring him a million cash by noon."

"Did he pay it?"

"Shit, he ain't have a choice. He had that new lil bad bitch he fuck with to drop it off. But fuck all that. Let me get to why he just dropped another ticket to get you up outta that jam."

And that was when Lil D told him: the old man Herb had made Weezy switch Princess and her friend Aqua over to QOD's highly coveted Prime Shift as the first part of some scheme to set up and murder a high-ranking member of the Traveling Vice Lords. No one knew why Herb had chosen Princess and Aqua to be a part of the sinister plot; that was what Weezy wanted Grind to find out.

Grind cleaned up the hair and stepped into the glassed-in shower, and while he stood barefoot on the marble floor, lathering himself with Dove body wash and rinsing off, he struggled with the idea of secretly working against the stunningly attractive woman he'd been dating for the past few weeks.

Princess Kelly was by far the most attractive woman he'd ever been intimate with. She reminded him of JT from the City Girls rap duo- thick and chocolate and as freaky as can be. She liked sitting her fat pussy on his mouth and coming all over his probing tongue. She liked sucking his dick until his cum shot out and clogged the back of her throat, and she always swallowed. She liked bending over and grabbing the back of her ankles while he beat up her pussy from the back, and he couldn't wait for the day when she allowed him to fuck her without a condom. His dick began to harden as he envisioned her creamy juices gathering along the length of his girthy ten inches. He stroked himself for a couple of seconds, and then the corners of his mouth rose into a welcoming smile as he listened to the subtle squeak of the bathroom door swinging open. Princess slid open the shower door and stepped inside, wearing nothing but a black shower cap, her icy new Cuban-link necklace and name pendant, and a white diamond Cartier watch.

"I ain't even gon' lie," she said, "That twenty-minute wait was too much for me. I need that dick right the fuck now. I've been waiting almost three weeks already."

Grind chuckled aloud and slipped an arm around her narrow waist, pulling her close. He kissed her delicately soft lips and filled his hands with her perfect sphere of an ass. She took his semi-erect phallus in both hands and gently began to pull on it. The more passionate their kisses became, the harder and longer his dick grew. He rubbed two wet fingertips on her clitoris until it felt as hard as his erection.

"Mmm," she moaned.

Grind took hold of her elbow and turned her away from him. He closed his hand around the nape of her neck and shoved her head forward bending her over. He rubbed the bulbous crown of his dick between her slippery vaginal lips and then slowly eased it inside of her.

"Fo'nem in the county thought I was lying when I said I was fuckin' on you," he said, running one hand up the center of her back as he slid in another couple of inches. "Told them niggas I don't do no capping. You my bitch. One of the baddest bitches in the city, and you picked one of the realest niggas."

Princess squealed as he started fucking her. His dick glided in and out between her fat round butt cheeks. He smacked her on the ass and squeezed the back of her neck. He'd been fantasizing about fucking her again ever since the day of his arrest. He'd jacked off to those fantasies eight or nine times when his cellmate wasn't around. Grind had fucked some bad bitches over the years, but none of them had come anywhere close to being as sexy and popular as Princess Kelly.

A gray marble bench ran along the back wall of the shower. Grind walked Princess forward until she planted her hands in the seat of the bench, and for a while there was nothing but the low pattering of warm water hitting the black marble floor, the much louder smack-smack-smack of skin colliding with skin, and the carnal moans and yelps of pleasure that escaped Princess's pretty mouth every couple of seconds.

A thoughtful smile crept across Grind's face as he eyed the white diamond Cuban-link Princess had clasped around her neck, and the blinging watch on her wrist. He had a baddie with her own cash. According to Lil D, Weezy had given Princess and Aqua the necklaces as part of their initiation into Prime Shift, which meant that technically Grind was slamming his oversized dick in and out of a real Prime Time Girl, and there wasn't one street nigga in the entire city of Chicago who didn't want to fuck the everlasting shit out of the Prime Time Girls. All of them were Instagram famous strippers/models with perfect bodies, gorgeous faces, and hundreds of thousands of devoted followers. Most of them dated pro athletes, superstar recording artists, and trap niggas who sold more bricks than Big Meech. Grind had about three hundred thousand dollars to his name, but he knew that being with Princess was the ultimate come up. He turned her around to face him and laid her on the bench. He pushed her thick brown legs up near her head and kissed the bottom of her foot as he pounded her pussy in the missionary position. Her bouncing titties and open-mouthed moans mesmerized him. He leaned in, pressed his lips to hers, and said, "I might be in love witcho lil sexy ass already."

Princess responded by digging her claws into his ribs and creaming over the length of his steadily thrusting erection. He looked down and nodded arrogantly at the sight of her copious juices on his dick. She felt hot, tight and gushy down there. He could feel her vaginal muscles contracting around his rigid pole as she tensed up and moaned her way through an orgasm, and he didn't slow down at all. His thrusts were relentless. He was still pounding her out seven minutes later when he felt the tingle in his scrotum that signaled an imminent eruption. Not wanting it to end, he pulled out of Princess and went to his knees, positioning her upright so that her back was against the black marble wall and her legs were parted with her creamy pink pussy spread open right in front of his mouth. He used two fingers to push back the hood of her clitoris and sucked the pink nub into his mouth, assaulting it with his tongue while thrusting two fingers inside of her.

"Oh shit," Princess said breathlessly. "I'm about to come again!"

"Mmm hmm," Grind hummed with his lips sealed around her clit.

Princess caressed the deep waves in Grind's hair as he looked up at the glistening white diamonds in her name pendant and the two beautiful brown breasts it rested between. There was a big diamond encrusted crown on the top left side of the letter P. Grind found himself wondering how much cash Weezy had dropped on the necklace. Then his gaze descended to her tight abdomen, and he eyed the dark oval shaped birthmark next to her navel. God, she was stunning.

Grind move down to the meaty lips of her pussy and ran the flat of his tongue between them, from the bottom all the way to the top. His tongue came away covered in a sweetly delectable cream, and he closed his mouth to savor the taste for a long moment before he swallowed it down and went back for seconds all the while utilizing one rapidly moving thumb to stimulate her swollen clitoris. His unrelenting ministrations elicited a high-pitched yelp from Princess.

"I'm coming," she said.

Still working his thumb on her clitoris, Grind rose to his feet and shoved his dick back into her creamy opening as the orgasm took hold of her, and he fucked her hard for fifty-one more seconds. Then he snatched himself out of her, and furiously stroking his erection and took aim at her pretty face just as she was coming down from the climactic high. She opened her mouth and extended her notably lengthy tongue. A slimy white rope of semen rocketed to the back of her throat. A second rope of goo shot out and left a serpentine design across her nose, lips, and chin. Before more of the slime could paint her face, she took his dick in one hand swallowing down the rest of his cum in three short gulps.

Grind stared down at her as she pulled and squeezed on his erratically twitching organ, his eyes roaming from the cum on her sexy brown face to the ice around her slender brown neck.

"Where you get this necklace from?" He knew the answer, but he figured asking about the Cuban-link and name pendant was the best way to broach the subject of her switch to Prime Shift.

"Long story," Princess said, smacking his deflating phallus off her lips. "But to make it short, Weezy moved me to Prime Shift last night. He gives all the girls these necklaces when they switch over to Prime. I'll probably be onstage when Megan Thee Stallion performs tonight."

Grind's eyebrows went high. "Yeah?" Then, wanting her to explain more, he said, "What made him move you to Prime Shift?"

The sexy look in Princess's eyes left in an instant. She averted her gaze and stood up. Stepped beneath the hot spray of water to rinse the slime from her pretty face. "I really don't want to talk about it," she said, after a time. "I honestly don't have an answer to that question anyway. It's what I've been trying to figure out myself?"

"Why you say that?"

Princess craned her neck and squinted at him. Then she shrugged her shoulders, sucked her teeth, and looked away. "I don't know. I truly don't know what to think. He just came at us out of nowhere with it. Called us up to his office and gave us these necklaces and fifty bands apiece. Bunny just called and gave me some info that cleared things up a little, but I'm still in the dark as to why I'm involved in all this bullshit. I'll figure it out, though. You better believe that."

Princess cleaned her pussy and left the shower, and Grind stared wantonly at her bouncy round butt cheeks as she dried off.

"Some bitches might try to give you some attention to get back at me," she said, adjusting her necklace. "Please do your best to ignore them. No matter how young, thick and pretty they might look, they'll only want you for one thing, and that's to get under my skin. I haven't even started working Prime Shift yet, and those Prime Time bitches are already hating."

"I'm with you, baby. Fuck them other bitches. If I fuck another bitch, it's gon' be a threesome with me and you. Like I told you when we first started fuckin' around, I'm tryna wife you. It's way too many grimy hoes out here in these streets. Too many cut-throat bitches who'll set a nigga up for a lil bit of nothing. I'm about loyalty. As long as you keep it a buck with me, I'ma do the same with you."

Princess smiled as she took off the shower cap and fixed her hair in the mirror. Her name fit her perfectly. She bore a striking resemblance to Bernice Burgas, an angelic pecan-brown visage with cute little baby hairs bordering her hairline; perky C-cup breasts that sat up evenly on her chest; a flat tummy and slim waistline that made her vastly sloping hips and ass even more visually appealing.

"Just make sure when you buy me that ring it's worth something," she said smilingly. "I got some money for you if you need it."

"I got my own money." Grind shut off the water and stepped out onto the Louis Vuitton rug, drying himself and thinking about the situation between Weezy and the old man, Herb. "I need you to drop me off at my sister's crib. I'ma jump in my truck and bend some blocks, collect some bread from a few niggas who been duckin' my people."

Princess shook her head disapprovingly. "No, I'm staying with you. And I don't want you driving your truck. You shot two gang members three weeks ago, and you know they're probably out looking for you. They don't know my car. And I have my conceal to carry license, so you don't have to ride dirty. I can shoot legally."

It was Grind's turn to smile. *"Whatever I do for Weezy,"* he thought to himself, *"I ain't turning on this bad lil bitch. I'll say fuck Weezy and ride out with her first."*

Chapter 16

The two hip surgeries Herb underwent in 2004 and 2013 had added a peculiar limp to his gait. Sometimes he exaggerated the limp to gain sympathy from others, or to make it seem like the cane he walked with was more of a necessity than a deadly weapon. When his blacked-out Bentley Mulsanne pulled to the curb outside of *Great Aunt Micky's*—the most popular black owned soul food restaurant in all of Chicago, located downtown in the exclusive Gold Coast shopping district—Herb's calculating gaze was everywhere at once, studying pedestrians and drivers alike. He'd recently had the cataracts removed from his eyes, giving him the clear vision he hadn't had in decades. His black Giorgio Armani suit and tie was tailored to his liking. The black alligator-skin Mauri shoes he wore fit him comfortably. He'd gotten two or three spots of blood on the toe of one shoe. Tiffany "T" Pires, the model-esque woman who'd sat to his left at the table inside of Queen of Diamonds, had used a small amount of diluted bleach to get rid of the blood.

T got from behind the steering wheel and pulled open Herb's door. He took his time climbing out of the backseat, looking around, steadying himself on his cane. The gears in his head were grinding away. The designer duffle bag in the trunk of his Bentley sedan contained ten thousand hundred-dollar bills, all of it bundled into *bank new* $10,000 packets. One million dollars.

The two young dark-skinned women flanked him as he entered the restaurant. The second woman's name was Tylisha Cooper, and since she and Tiffany were best friends, the two of them were often referred to as T and T, or TNT, which couldn't have been a more fitting name because they were the bomb. The kind of women Herb and his fellow Vietnam soldiers had taped to their bunks and masturbated to during the sixteen year war. He'd first met Tylisha two years ago at Redbone's, a strip club on the city's west side. He'd paid her a thousand dollars for a one night stand, and once she'd seen that he was financially loaded and living like a king in his Berwyn home she'd stuck around, introducing her friend to him a few weeks later. She'd been staying at one of his south side rental properties when she captured the video of Weezy murdering his ex-wife's abusive lover, and she hadn't told Herb about the video until two weeks ago when they were reclined in comfortably cushion lounge chairs behind the Belmond Copacabana Palace in Rio de Janeiro sipping caipirinhas and enjoying a memorable view of the Brazilian sunset. In the fourteen days since Tylisha first showed him the video, Herb had conspired with his nephew, Baby Stone to not only extort Weezy out of a few million dollars, but also to use the ruthless killer to take out the one man they both wanted dead.

Thirty-seven year old Baby Stone was seated in the exclusive Red Room section in the back of GAM's. He'd called ahead and reserved two table for their lunch meeting, and when Herb sat down across from him, he looked up and regarded the old man with a brief, gregarious grin.

"I like that hat," Baby Stone said.

He was light-skinned like his mother and nearly as thin as Herb, dressed in a black and red Gucci jogger over matching sneakers. A pair of gold-framed Dior sunglasses concealed his studious brown eyes. He'd taken a few bites from the Cajun-style beef sirloin steak and lobster on the plate before him and was chewing as he spoke.

"You got something in your hand."

Baby Stone motioned toward Herb's left hand as the two girls were seated at a table with the two younger gang members who acted as his security. Herb looked at the palm of his hand, noticed a dried splash of blood and shrugged his shoulders indifferently.

"Shit happens," he said. "That guy Weezy reached for my throat. Lost his hand in the process."

He picked up a plush white napkin, licked one corner of it, and wiped the blood from his hand.

"He's fine though. He'll live. I told him about Markio, and that's all that matters. We've set the wheels of destiny in motion. Now all we do is sit back and wait."

Baby Stone nodded his head and drank from his ice-cold glass of lemonade, and as he did it, Herb ruminated over the circumstances that had led them to this headache of an extortion scheme to begin with.

It had all started with Baby Stone, who for years had been a respected General for the Black P. Stones in Hyde Park, responsible for overseeing the street gang's activities and supplying them with drugs and guns for distribution throughout their south side neighborhood. A millionaire several times over, Baby Stone and his close friend Veemo had managed their territory with brute force, ordering their foot soldiers to gun down their rivals—namely the Hobos and the "Fifth Ward" Black Disciples—in brazen broad-day shootings.

Herb's involvement with the Black P. Stones went back half a century, from the mid-seventies, in the days when the gang's founder, Jeff Fort, known within the gang as Chief Malik, was still wreaking havoc on the streets of Chicago. Herb had declined Chief Malik's offer to become an official member of the gang, but he'd always maintained close ties with its original members and their descendants. Over the past fifty years or so he'd played a significant role in the logistics of the gang's drug empire. He'd gone from flying out to New York to negotiate multi-ton heroin shipments with Frank Lucas in the 1970's to doing the same thing with Mexico's Matamoros drug cartel just a couple of months ago. Herb was both a beloved military veteran and a man of importance in the criminal underworld. Every man who'd ever posed a threat to his close knit circle of friends and family had been hastily eliminated. Which was why he was after Millionaire Markio, the New York times bestselling crime novelist who recently offered a million dollars to any man or woman who could locate and kill Herb's beloved nephew, Baby Stone.

"You still haven't told me what happened between you and that writer," Herb said, cutting into his own sixteen ounce steak. "What made him put a million dollars on your head? That's a shitload of money, even to someone like him. You have to had done something."

Baby Stone was silent for a long moment, chewing, nodding his head, staring down at his plate. He looked a lot like his father, Jesse Harris Sr., had looked in his younger years, long before the colon cancer had ravaged his striking features, leaving him ashen, emaciated and ultimately dead at the tender age of 58.

"He fronted me some work," Baby Stone said, after a time. Then he shrugged and added, "Well, a lot of work. Four hundred twenty bricks of the purest cocaine to hit the city in years. I paid the nigga two million up front. Owed him the other eight point five."

"So, what happened?" Herb inquired.

Baby Stone hesitated. He snatched a glance at his diamond drizzled Patek Philippe wristwatch, licked his thin lips and shook his head.

"I ain't gon' lie," he said finally. "I said fuck that nigga, I ain't about to pay him no eight and a half million dollars. You heard what Plies said. *Ran off on the plug twice. He steady callin', I ain't callin' back.* I'm keepin' all that shit. If he wanna war about it, we can war about it. I ain't never like them Travelers no way."

Herb squinted his ancient brown eyes at his younger brother's only son. He'd never heard of anyone called Plies, but he knew legions of Traveling Vice Lords. He'd known Neal Wallace Jr, the King of the TVLs personally, and had done business with him on a number of occasions.

"So," he said, leaning forward a couple of inches, "You mean to tell me we're going through all of this for no reason other than you being greedy! Are you fucking kidding me?"

"Look, I got an expensive lifestyle to maintain," Baby Stone explained. "I got three different condos here in the city, seven foreign cars, two baby mommas, three kids, and a fiancé to take care of. I got a construction company and a landscaping business to manage. And on top of all of that, I got the streets to feed. I gotta supply the Moes with guns, dope, bond money, cars, and all kinds of other shit. Eight and a half million dollars is a lot of money to just give up. I'd rather run off on that nigga and have some of the Moes slide down on him with four or five Dracos. I know he got a bunch of security, and I know it'll be hard to get at him, but shit…fuck it. One way or other, I'm keepin' the twenty million I made off that flip."

Another dismissive shrug from Jesse James Harris, Jr. Herb's frustrated squint became more stringent. His heartbeat hastened within the confines of his seemingly undernourished chest. He sat back in his chair and forced himself to calm down a bit. He didn't speak for another 15 seconds, and when he did it was in a lower, more controlled tone of voice.

"Fine," Herb said, nodding his head defeatedly and using the blood-smeared napkin to dab a few beads of perspiration from the deep creases of his brow. "But you might want to lay low. There are a lot of gangsters who won't hesitate to shoot you and your two henchmen when the payoff's a million in cash. Get out of the city for the next couple of months. Weezy and his boys are gonna take care of Markio when he goes to Queen of Diamonds to celebrate his birthday on the 1st of February. He's already posted a flyer for the party on social media."

One corner of Baby Stone's narrow lips ascended in a triumphant little smirk. It was the same expression his late father had put on whenever he won a debate against the great Herbert Harris.

"Might be hard to talk my fiancée into leaving town for a few months." Baby Stone snapped off a juicy bite of lobster tail. "She's making good money at that designer boutique she just opened in Hyde Park. And you know I gotta keep an eye on Princess for Veemo. Bro would kill me if I let anything happen to her or Vee."

This elicited a barely audible sigh from Herb. Baby Stone's best friend was a fellow Black P. Stone named Vonzale, but everyone called him Veemo because his original nickname had been Vee and also because the Stones were often referred to as Moes due to their deeply rooted connections with the Moorish Science Temple of America and the Moroccan community. It was Baby Stone who'd pressured Herb into making Weezy move Princess and her friend Aqua to Prime Shift. Millionaire Markio followed Princess and Aqua on every one of their social media platforms. Baby Stone had suggested that using them as pawns to reel in the notoriously trigger happy Vice Lord was the easiest way to ensnare him in their trap. Even if Princess and Aqua didn't succeed in luring Markio in, it would still be a win for them, because they would be making a lot more money as Prime Shift girls and a win for Princess was technically a win for Baby Stone, since she was the mother of his best friend's daughter.

Over the next few minutes, Herb and Baby Stone ate their meals in silence, while at the next table, Tiffany and Tylisha engaged in flirty conversations with Mike Moe, and L-Stone, the two large men who were never far from Baby Stone's side. They were dressed just like him, in heavy designer winter gear and sparkling diamond jewelry. Herb didn't much care for that thuggish sort of attire. His two female companions could easily be mistaken for congresswomen or fresh-faced attorneys from some high-priced Chicago law firm. Herb had rescued them from the slums and introduced them to the good life. In the short time they'd known him, the two young women had already become the unashamedly proud owners of nine neatly maintained rental properties, including a 48 unit apartment building on the north side of the city that brought in $96,000 a month.

"I'll tell you this," Herb said, after a while. A note of finality darkened his gravelly tone as he said it. "You owe me a million in cash for this little stunt. I'll take care of this whole ordeal, but once it's said and done, you owe."

Baby Stone let out an amused chuckle, but he quickly choked it off after seeing the unsettling seriousness in his uncle's tight eyed expression.

"Chill out, unc," he said. "Learn to live a little."

"You keep moving the way you're moving," Herb warned, "You won't have much more living to do. And you can take that straight to the bank."

Chapter 17

Bunny XXX's quivering mouth was stretched open as wide as her asshole and pussy were, and for a damned good reason. Tyrone Steele was behind her, holding her hips in both hands and sliding his lengthy Black Mamba in and out of her lubricated rectum, while beneath her Brick Hart, another popular black porn actor, sat naked on the rich leather sofa smacking her on the ass and thrusting his nine-inch organ up into her dripping wet vagina.

The other two men stood on either side of Tyrone, jerking their rock-hard dicks, both of them eager to get inside of Bunny. One of them had briefly sat on the back of the sofa and allowed Bunny to suck him off for a couple of minutes, but her incomparable oral skills had nearly caused him to ejaculate prematurely, so he flipped backwards onto the floor behind the sofa in his haste to escape the iron grip of her noisily sucking mouth, leading to a porn blooper the director had laughingly sworn would be included in the final edits.

Bunny's new boyfriend had arrived in his snow-white Rolls-Royce Cullivan a little over an hour ago. He was a short, handsome, light-skin gangster of a man who'd never done a porn scene in his life, but he enjoyed watching his woman in action. This was his 5th time visiting the set during the filming of one of her scenes, and his first time seeing her with more than one man. He sat near Noble in one of the director's chairs, typing on his laptop computer looking up every now and then to gawk at the impossibly long erection that had been pounding away at Bunny's slippery asshole for more than ten minutes now.

His name was Markio Earl, but millions of urban fiction readers knew him as Millionaire Markio, the award-winning author behind a slew of bestselling street lit novels that were as captivatingly realistic and vividly descriptive as any Stephen King saga. Markio was also a high-ranking gang member and a low-key drug kingpin who'd raked in at least 100 million in the last year alone. His books were real because his life was real. It was this less known part of him that had attracted Bunny to Markio from the very start back when he and world-renowned attorney Nikkia Staples were still dating. Bunny was pretty sure that Markio and his gang were behind the kidnapping of her friend, Whitney Clarrett, the woman Markio had dated for a short time after his release from prison a few years ago, but Bunny had fallen too deeply for him to care about anything in his past. He was one of the few men in her life who loved her unconditionally despite her sexually promiscuous career choice, and for that she loved him deeply, which is why she sent him a text message while the assistants were busy applying body oil to her meaty ass and thighs.

"I need you to meet me at this gangbang shoot. It's urgent."

She sent him the location of the 16,000 square feet suburban mansion, and he'd arrived in his Cullivan forty minutes late, trailed closely by a Rolls-Royce Phantom and two Jeep Grand Cherokee Trailhawks of the same color. The gang members who'd accompanied him here were gathered in another room toward the rear of the mansion, smoking paunchy blunts of exotic marijuana and drinking from Styrofoam cups full of ice cream soda and Wockhardt Promethazine with Codeine syrup. Bunny had walked past and seen them watching an NBA game during the two minute break she'd taken from filming. She'd taken advantage of those two minutes to give Markio a quick rundown of everything she'd learned from Big Gabby. He listened intently, keeping his lips sealed shut and his ears wide open, and he hadn't uttered a single word as she turned and sauntered back toward the living room in her plush pink Versace robe. He returned to his chair and continued typing on his MacBook Pro, occasionally pausing to look up and watch Tyrone Steele and three other well-endowed men penetrate Bunny vaginally and anally.

Her heated moans only intensified when she looked back over her shoulder and caught Markio watching her. She ogled the phallus print of an erection along the inner thigh of his fitted Balmain jeans and smiled a little when she realized she was turning him on. For a few seconds she thought of Weezy and wondered how Markio would ultimately respond to the threat against his life, but then Tyrone drove in deep, knocking the breath from her lungs, and after that all she could think about was the huge black penis that seemed to be reaching way up in the center of her chest. A legitimate orgasm seized her ten seconds later. She wrapped her arms around Brick Hart's cornrowed head and practically screamed as the two men continued their merciless assault on her lubricious love tunnels, and as soon as the orgasm passed the director ended the shoot by having Bunny kneel between the four men as they masturbated and ejaculated all over her face and into her open mouth. She appreciated the gooey, bitter taste of so much semen splashing across her extended tongue, but she was careful not to swallow any of it. Ther was only one man whose cum she was fond of swallowing, and his name was Markio.

Afterward, Bunny rose to her feet with an ingratiating smile on her cum splattered face, scooped up her purse, and allowed a cameraman to follow her to the same bathroom she'd used before the shoot. She shut the door on the camera, used the sink to clean her face and spit out her mouthful of goo, then settled into the warm bubble bath an assistant had prepared for her beforehand. She was sitting up in the bathtub, still recovering from the sexual bliss she'd experienced at the hands of her four male colleagues when Markio entered the bathroom and sat down on the lid of the smart toilet across the room from her. He wore a cool smirk on his intriguingly serious light-brown visage. The furry white Chanel skullcap on his head was titled leftward, and it matched his thick white Chanel sweater and the plain white Louboutin sneakers on his feet. He wore half a dozen diamond necklaces, two of them thick Cuban-links with brilliantly glistening white diamond pendants hanging down from them. One pendant spelled out *Millionaire Markio*. The other was a large five-pointed star with the *DST* stretched across it in bold diamond lettering. He had his titanium iPhone in one hand, but he wasn't on it. The screen was off. He was a short, stocky gangster who reminded Bunny of Yo Gotti, her favorite gangster rapper of all time, and just like Yo Gotti, Millionaire Markio really lived the life he spoke of in his art.

"Will you hand me my phone?" Bunny asked. "It's in my purse."

Markio gave a subtle nod. He got up from the smart toilet, fished around her Birkin, and came out with her phone which was identical to his. He handed it to her and went back to his seat on the cushioned toilet lid.

"I might need you to get me Weezy's home address," he said and shook his head regretfully. "Damn. That's my nigga. Hate to have to fuck bro over like that."

"I'm not sure where he lives. He bought a big ass mansion somewhere out in Naperville a few months ago, but Big Gabby said he's getting that one renovated, so he has to be staying somewhere else."

Her words slowed as she began gazing over a group chat one of the QOD strippers had started some months back. Twenty-nine girls were currently engaged in the chat, and it didn't take long for Bunny to figure out what had gone down.

"Oh my God!" She gasped and flicked her eyes in Markio direction. "Somebody just cut Weezy's hand off! Right in the middle of the club this morning!"

Markio furrowed his brow and got up to take a look at the group chat on Bunny's phone screen, but she was already telling him what it said before he could get close enough to read it himself.

"Some old man with a walking stick came in with two dark-skinned girls and sat down at one of the front tables. Weezy went over to talk with the man, they had some words, and next thing you know the old man whipped a sword out of his walking stick and chopped Weezy's hand right off. Two of the bouncers rushed him to the hospital. Oh, my God. This is crazy."

Markio took her phone and spent a long silent moment reading over the chat thread. When he gave it back, he squinted and nodded, holding his chin between thumb and forefinger. The flawless white diamonds in his five-pointed star pinkie ring twinkled like a star-spangled sky on a cloudless night.

"It had to be that old man Gabby said was trying to extort Weezy into getting you killed," Bunny surmised. She was scrubbing her skin with a soapy towel, fingering her holes, hurrying to cleanse herself and get out of the tub so she could get going.

"What was that old man's name?" Markio asked, pulling a Glock handgun with an extended magazine from behind the buckle of his Chanel belt and yanking the slide back to chamber a round.

Bunny's eyes got big. "I don't know. Gabby didn't say. I'll call back and ask her when I get outta this tub."

Markio shook his head. "Nah. Hell nah."

He went to the door and locked it, and when he returned to stand over Bunny with his gun in hand she thought she sensed a clearly discernible threat behind his cool brown eyes.

"You gon' call Big Gabby right now."

Chapter 18

Five of the Prime Time Girls met up for a late lunch at Cherish Taylor's 7,500 square foot Royalty Suite on the 44th floor of the famed Costilla Hotel & Tower. Cherish Taylor, Shmoney Rose, Sasha the Stallion, Thick Doll, and Kimmy Kakes. Kimmy and Thick Doll arrived together in Thick Doll's matte red Lamborghini Urus. They left the $300,000 dollar luxury SUV with the valet and entered the glorious steel and glass skyscraper with two bodyguards in tow mere seconds before Sasha's sky blue Rolls-Royce Ghost and Shmoney's hot pink Bentayga pulled up in front of the building.

The wintry air was cold enough to stun the senses, but the girls only suffered a few brutal seconds of it. Their heavy fur coats denied the frigid breeze of entry, and then their high-heeled designer boots landed on heated white marble flooring as the ten foot glass doors swung shut behind them. They gathered in an elevator, Kimmy and Thick Doll whispering about the shocking news of Weezy losing his hand in the mid-morning sword attack inside Queen of Diamonds, Sasha and Shmoney discussing the scandalous affair that had taken place in the backseat of Shmoney's Bentley truck last night. Their gossip mongering tapered off when the elevator doors slid open before them, because Cherish was standing there in her doorway holding her hips and glowing like the rich bitch she was in a Burberry catsuit over open-toed Jimmy Choo stiletto heels.

"PTG in this hoe!" Cherish shrieked joyously.

She stuck out her tongue, grabbed her knees, and bounced her fat round ass to the beat of a Fendi Da Rapper song she had blaring from her sound system. The other girls started twerking with her. After all, at the end of the day, the five of them were just a clique of ordinary project chicks who'd capitalized off their strikingly attractive looks to rub shoulders with the rich and famous, and their tactics had paid off handsomely.

Ten minutes later all five of them were seated around one end of a long Egyptian mahogany dining table capable of seating nine others. Their lunch, a photogenic combination of pasta, seafood, salads, and fruits had been prepared by an elite team of culinary masters in the Michelin starred Papi's restaurant that took up most of the five star hotel's fifth floor. The girls posed in their seats while Cherish's 19-year-old sister Brazilia snapped a few dozen photos of them for their social media pages, and then they got down to business.

"First things first," Cherish said, casually adjusting her Cuban link necklace. "I don't know what the hell that whole situation with Weezy was about. Somehow they allowed a 100 year old man to just waltz in and cut his whole goddamn hand off."

"That's exactly what the fuck he get switching them musty hoes over to Prime Shift without telling nobody," Shmoney spat venomously. "God don't like ugly."

Thick Doll said, "That's neither here nor there. The question is, how the hell did they let that man in there with a whole sword? And they say one of the girls pulled a gun from inside her purse when Fat Perry and Adonis went at them. How did she sneak that in?"

"Big Gabby just fired the doorman," Kimmy Kakes said. "She reviewed the cameras and saw that old man slip him a stack of hundreds to turn off the metal detector. You know the AI technology in those Panneton cameras allows them to zoom in really close. Gabby peeped the whole play."

"I hope this shit doesn't fuck up our money tonight," Sasha complained as she stuck a fork full of pasta in her mouth.

Kimmy stuck out her bottom lip and shook her head. "I don't think it will. Gabby shut the club down for a couple of hours, but that's only because two customers called the police when they saw Weezy get his hand cut off. The doors should be back open before Preferred Shift starts. Hospitalized or not, Weezy ain't about to miss no money."

Both Cherish and Shmoney Rose rolled their pretty eyes and fluttered their false eyelashes at the mere mention of Preferred Shift. It was the shift they considered beneath them. Never mind the fact that every single one of QOD's seventeen Prime Shift dancers had paid their Preferred Shift dues, and that several of them still worked the Preferred Shift on certain nights, just as Sasha had done last night, and Kimmy had done three nights before. Cherish and Shmoney were without question the most boujie, conceited women in the crew, and knowing that Princess and Aqua had gone from Preferred to Prime without anyone informing the two of them had them on ten.

A vast collection of alcoholic beverages lined the shelves behind Cherish's wet bar. Thick Doll sent Brazilia over to grab a bottle of Dussé cognac and a stack of crystal ball glasses. Thick Doll poured herself a full glass and passed the bottle over to Kimmy, who shot her a fleeting look that said she was also in dire need of a drink. Both of them had taken a liking to Princess a long time ago. She was a bad, young hood bitch who didn't take bullshit from anybody, and Thick Doll knew for a fact that no one in the room would have the guts to speak ill of Princess to her face. Princess was known for beating bitches down. Veemo, her baby's father, was a south side legend who'd taken his time like a man when he was arrested for dealing half a kilo of cocaine to an informant; and it was rumored that Princess had played a part in the informant's murder five months later.

Thick Doll had her own ties to Veemo's gang of Hyde Park Black P. Stones. Her eight year old son's father was Baby Stone, the General of the gang and Veemo's right hand man. Baby Stone hadn't lain in bed with her in a couple of years, but he still provided for her and his son as if they'd never broken up. He given her $300,000 in cash to purchase her Lamborghini Urus and the $450,000 she used to launch her home health care business. He'd paid for her fat transfer surgery, her breast augmentations, and the liposuction she'd had done six months ago. Just last week he'd visited Queen of Diamonds with several other members of his gang, and he'd thrown more than $150,000 in hundred dollar bills at Thick Doll, BunnyXXX, and Shmoney Rose, layering the VIP Lounge floor in crisp new Benjamins. That being said, Thick Doll felt a special connection to Princess. The father of their children was like brothers, so Thick Doll had been looking forward to forming a sisterly bond with Princess. Seeing the obvious distaste with which Shmoney Rose and Cherish Taylor spoke of Princess grated on Thick Doll's nerves like fingernails on a chalkboard. The more Dussé she consumed, the more Thick Doll was tempted to say something in Princess' defense.

"So," Sasha asked, "how are we supposed to deal with Aqua and Princess? Are we welcoming them in or what? I need to know."

"Of course we're welcoming them in," Kimmy said, rather sharply.

At 34, she was the oldest woman in the crew, a bad redbone with generous curves, the face of an angel, and the ferocious attitude of a feral pit bull. "We welcomed all the other bitches, didn't we? We welcomed Bunny, and those big booty white bitches and Asian bitches. I didn't hear anybody debating whether we should accept them when they got moved to Prime."

"Yeah, but that's different," Cherish argued.

She was leaning back in her leather upholstered chair at the head of the table while Brazilia filled her glass with cognac.

"All 17 Prime Time Girls paid their dues beforehand. Weezy was forced to put these two new bitches on Prime. Somebody's trying to extort him. Hell, it might even be the same man who cut off his hand, and whoever it is demanded that Princess and Aqua be moved to Prime Shift. Those aren't exactly the kind of bitches we should be inviting into our circle."

"Period," Shmoney agreed. "Ain't no telling what kinda bullshit they on. For all we know, they could be working with the enemy."

Thick Doll drank from her glass and said nothing. She could feel the liquid anger boiling deep down in the pit of her stomach. According to her Illinois driver's license, she was a 25-year-old black woman named Karionna Patrice Washington, which explained why the majority of her family and friends still referred to her as Kari. She was a product of Chicago's west side, one of the many ghetto girls who'd been raised in the blighted Rockwell Gardens Apartment complex. Most of her family still resided on the west side, in a section of the K-Town neighborhood that for decades had been ruled over by the Conservative Vice Lords.

Before becoming a famous stripper with almost four million TikTok followers, Thick Doll had made a living trafficking bricks of cocaine and heroin from Baby Stone's gang in Hyde Park to the CVLs her stepfather, Yella Man ran with in K-Town. Back in those days, Thick Doll had been considered a serious threat to other bitches. Just three years ago when she was just and aspiring cosmetologist with a killer body and a gorgeous smile, she pulled a baby Glock from her purse and shot Baby Stone's other baby mama, Shayna, twice in the gut for disrespecting her on Instagram, and when seven of Shayna's cousins tried jumping her at a house party two months later, she'd drawn that same subcompact pistol and emptied its ten round clip into the side door they attempted to flee through, striking one girl in the right buttock, a second girl in the left elbow and lower back, and a third through the right earlobe.

Looking across the table at Cheris and Shmoney, Thick Doll found herself seeing red, just like she had the night of that house party. She'd had a lot of good times with Cherish Taylor, but they were both alpha females and they butted heads quite often. Shmoney Rose wasn't a factor. She was really just Cherish's echo, agreeing with any and everything Cherish had to say. It was pretty much the same situation with Sasha.

"Princess and Aqua might not even know about what's going on with Weezy," Kimmy opined. "Has anyone even asked them?"

"Nope," said Shmoney. "Gabby don't want us telling them either. We don't need to ask them hoes nothin' anyway. I fucked the shit outta Aqua's man last night, and I'ma do it again. And if she got anything to say about it, I'ma slap the taste out her mouth. Simple as that."

"That part," Cherish said with an amused chuckle as she reached over and high-five Shmoney Rose. "I fucked the nigga that was supposed to be linking with Princess today. Had him in my bed all night and all this morning. I know she big mad."

Thick Doll sucked her teeth and regarded Cherish with an icy stare. Unable to maintain her silence for a moment longer, she rolled her eyes and said, "See, that's that shit I don't like. You messy bitches ain't got no reason to hate on Princess or Aqua. Y'all reachin' hard, trying to find any reason to put another black woman down instead of helping lift her up. And you know what?" She poked a forefinger at the air, first in Cherish's direction, then toward Shmoney. "Ain't neither one of you scary hoes gon' be bold enough to pop off on Princess when she walks into that club tonight. Y'all know it like I know it. That girl is one of the Lady Moes from Hyde Park, She'll fuck around and shoot both of you ignorant bitches, and if she wanna keep her hands clean, you better believe she won't hesitate to pay somebody else to do it for her."

The right corner of Cherish's upper lip twitched. Her jaw muscles flexed as she clenched her teeth. The movements were subtle, but Thick Doll noticed them, nonetheless. She was unfazed by the expression. A part of her wished Cherish *would* get up and come after her. She'd been looking for a reason to break her foot off in Cherish ass for months now, and there was no better time than the present.

"Uhmm," Cherish said, fluttering her long eyelashes again. "I don't know what done got into you, but I ain't got time for it today. Kimmy will you take her somewhere? Anywhere but here. Please and thank you."

Thick Doll downed the rest of her drink in a single gulp and stood to leave. "I've been kicked out of better places," she said, snatching a glance at the four giant bodyguards who escorted them up to the suite. "I'll see you scary ass hoes tonight. I'll be the one hugging and welcoming Princess and Aqua into the squad, showing them around the PTG locker room. You know, the kind of shit real bitches do. And if any one of y'all got a problem with that, I'll be the one slapping the taste out of your mouths. Period."

Kimmy stifled a laugh as she got up to put on her flashy red mink coat. "Deuces, y'all," she said, and threw up the peace sign.

A Secure Force bodyguard named Donell led them onto the elevator chuckling and shaking his head all the way there.

Thick Doll said, "I can't stand that fake ass bitch."

"Me either." Kimmy shrugged. "But fuck that hoe. We'll welcome the new girls with open arms, and if the rest of PTG don't like it, all them hoes can eat a dick."

Chapter 19

When Princess pulled her Mercedes to the curb in front of Grind's sister Vanessa Rose's single-family home on 60th Street and Hermitage Avenue, nine members of Grind's family were standing on the front porch and in the open doorway, all of them clearly elated to see him free from the historically violent confines of Cook County Jail.

Grind was all smiles as he climbed out of the passenger's seat and into the outstretched arms of his relatives, but Princess remained vigilant. Growing up in Hyde Park, around a fearless army of Black P. Stones whose lives were constantly in danger from both opposing gang members and crooked CPD officers, she'd quickly learned the importance of keeping an eye out for potential threats.

Perhaps this was why she spotted the off-white Honda minivan full of young black men that was parked halfway down the block. She didn't see them until Grind was already out of the car hugging the two female children who'd sprinted down the porch steps to leap into his arms. The men in the van seemed to have already been watching Vanessa's house. Princess was suddenly reminded of KTS Dre, the underground Chicago rapper who was gunned down right in front of Cook County Jail as soon as he was released on house arrest. One of his fellow inmates had obviously contacted the shooter with the news of his imminent release, and now, with her unwavering stare focused solely on the minivan, Princess believed the same thing might happen Grind.

She reached under her thigh and took hold of her. 357 caliber Glock 32 pistol as the minivan's rear passenger side door was sliding open. Thinking ahead, she switched out the standard twelve round clip for and extended 30-round clip, and as she calmly pushed open her door and stepped out on to the street with her right hand buried in the Birkin purse hanging down from her shoulder, she stared right at the two men who emerged from the rear of the minivan holding miniature assault rifles in their gloved hands. They pulled black cotton ski masks down over their faces and came running up the middle of the street.

For three years before his unfortunate arrest, Veemo and his entourage of gang members had visited a shooting range in Lake Station, Indiana. He'd taken Princess with him on at least three dozen different occasions, and it hadn't taken her but seven or eight trips to start hitting the center of the bullseye on the head of the paper target. Just as she'd done at the shooting range, she calmed herself by taking in a couple of deep breaths as the two masked gunmen closed in, filling her lungs with cold December air. Just as they begin to raise their weapons, she drew hers, took aim at one man's forehead, and squeezed the trigger.

BOOM!

The man's masked head rocked backward, and as he was going down, as Vanessa and her two daughters screamed out in horror, and as Grind began to reach for his own pistol, Princess swung her gun to the right and fired again. The second gunman's head jerked more to the side than to the back, and he went down too, right beside his friend. His mini assault rifle went skittering several feet away. Princess noted the sliding weapon without looking at it. Her intense gaze flicked to the wide-eyed driver of the minivan. She kept her manicured finger on the trigger, ready to fire again if necessary but thoughtful enough to consider the probable ramifications of an unprovoked shooting. The two men she'd just dropped in the middle of the street were justifiable homicides. Shooting an unarmed driver might put her behind bars like Veemo.

The minivan rocketed away in reverse, swinging from side to side in the snow-slickened street and side-swiped an Audi SUV as it went. The three young men who stood on the porch with Vanessa also drew pistols, but Princess had eliminated the threat before anyone else could react.

"Damn baby," Grind said as he came around to stand next to her. "Where the hell you learn to aim like that? You good?"

"I'm fine. Get your family in the house and put up those guns." Princess took out her phone and reluctantly dialed 911. When the dispatcher picked up, Princess said, "Um, hello, this is Princess Kelly. I just shot two gunmen on Sixteenth and Hermitage. They tried to run up on me and my man. I'm pretty sure I killed them both."

Grind stared at Princess for a long moment, his eyes wide like the minivan driver's had been. Then he and his male relative hurried away to stash their illegal firearms mere seconds before the paranoia inducing sound of police sirens pierced the silence. Seconds later, two police cars rounded the corner onto Hermitage and Princess could only think of one thing: tonight, would be her first time ever clocking in for Prime Shift, and if she ended up being late because of this shooting, Big Gabby would likely slap her with another fine.

Chapter 20

"Okay, I don't know what else to tell you, boo. The man snuck in with a sword. There was no way I could've foreseen that happening, and there's no way for me to find out his name. You'll have to direct all your questions to Mr. Sullivan."

The two white male CPD detectives glanced at each other. Then, they turned their attention to Big Gabby and when she only stared at the computer that sat in front of her on Weezy's desk studying the very same cameras she'd just sworn were out of order at the time of the sword attack, the two burly police detectives spun around and left the office, nodding their head in what she took to be a threatening manner. Big Gabby looked up at them as they swaggered down the hallway. A bouncer escorted them to the elevators, and as soon as they were gone, he returned to the open doorway to check on Big Gabby.

His name was Bobby Kyles, so some of the girls called him Bobby, and nearly everyone else called him Bee Kay. At five-ten, he was among the shortest of QOD's bouncers, but he was two hundred and forty pounds, brawny and fit, and growing up around legendary K-Town CVLs Bullock and Pierre had made him a highly feared man. He had dreadlocks at the top and a fade around the back and sides of his head. His black, long-sleeved SECURITY shirt fit him like a second skin, accentuating his muscular dark arms and the six bricks of muscle that made up his abdomen. He was paid a hundred dollars per shift like the other QOD bouncers, but many of the dancers were known for tipping bouncers for keeping them safe, and several of them routinely slipped Bee Kay a few extra hundred when their shifts came to an end. He used the money to keep his wardrobe on point. His Dior jogging pants were probably worth a thousand dollars or more. The Nike Air Max sneakers he had on were rare and probably cost him five or six hundred. The small diamond cross that hung from his thin diamond necklace had cost him some thousands.

"Want me to go down there and make sure they leave?" Bee Kay asked.

Big Gabby shook her head no. "I can watch them from here."

"Heard anything from Weezy?"

"Not yet. I'm about to call his girlfriend's phone now. Bunny called me back a few minutes ago, but that was right when those cops walked in. I'm about to call Mikayla. She was in the hospital room with Weezy when I called earlier."

Bee Kay licked his lips and smiled. "Bunny so fuckin' bad. On the five, if it wasn't for my crazy ass baby mama, I would've been done fucked the shit outta her."

"She's doing a photoshoot with Tyrone Steele, that man with the fourteen inch dick. I am sooo jealous right now. I'd pay him fifty bands for some of that dick."

"*What?*" Bee Kay said, sounding seriously offended. "Man, I ain't tryna hear about no other nigga's dick. I'm gone."

He turned to leave, and Big Gabby laughed joyously as she watched him storm off down the blue carpeted hallway, pulling his smartphone from his pants pocket as he went. She raised her own phone from the desk, scrolled through her call log, and dialed Mikayla's number. The sexy young Chicago Heights native answered on the third ring.

"Yeah?"

"How's he doing?"

"They were able to reattach his hand. He's asleep right now. Doped up on morphine, you know. He said to tell you to make sure everything goes as planned tonight. He's trusting you to oversee Megan Thee Stallion's whole performance. You're to pay her a hundred grand up front and another hundred grand on the back end."

"I know how to run things. We'll be good. You just stay there and make sure he's okay. I'll be to see him as soon as I get up tomorrow morning. Call me if he needs anything."

Big Gabby ended the call. She had a large bag of Flamin' Hot Doritos and a cold 24 ounce bottle of Dr. Pepper open on the desk. She dug her free hand into the bag, took out four triangular chips, and bit down on them as she pushed them in her mouth. *Crunch, Crunch, Crunch.* She eyed the elevator cameras while she chewed. The cops were engaged in conversation. She accessed the intercom to listen in.

"...hiding something. Those are Panneton cameras. Those things are more high-tech than any other camera in existence. Make 4KHD and all the rest of today's technology look like ancient history. There's graphic, vivid footage of that man getting his hand hacked off. I'd bet my salary on it."

"I'll contact Walloby from the FBI's Street Gang Unit. Give him Sullivan's name and social. He can rot away in a cell with the likes of Jeff Fort and Larry Hoover. That bastard Weezy has more money than we could ever dream of having, and he's a gangster! He studied a how to book on cryptocurrency investments when bitcoins were hardly worth anything, and he invested an entire multi-million dollar settlement he'd won from a lawsuit he filed in prison. Turned it into somewhere around a hundred million and bought this strip club. And this a known gang member we're talking about here. Someone's going to die over his hand getting cut off. All we have to do is listen and watch. Get a warrant to eavesdrop on that phone of his before he orders the hit. That's conspiracy to commit murder all day."

"Precisely," said the CPD detective who was standing at the chromium panel of numbered buttons. "And we'll celebrate right here at Queen of Diamonds when we raid this slut fest."

Big Gabby muted the intercom and briefly considered making her irate voice boom from the heavens of that descending chrome box, but at the last moment she thought better of it. She kept her mouth shut, sneered at the two conniving policemen, and followed their every move on the cameras until they were out in the parking lot, slipping into their nondescript, dark blue Chevy Tahoe, and cruising away.

"You're out of your fucking minds if you think I'm going to let y'all just burn up my bag," Gabby said out loud. She went to her missed calls and thought about returning Bunny's call. Then, gulping down acidic mouthfuls of sweet bubbly soda, she decided against it and instead called the one man she should have called from the very start. Millionaire Markio.

Chapter 21

The motorcade of gaudy white vehicles began with Markio's older cousin, Buck's Jeep Grand Cherokee Trailhawk up front. Known in the street as a Trackhawk, the insanely fast SUV had become a staple among rich black gangsters over the past couple of years due to its ability to both escape shooting scenes and evade law enforcement. Buck and his close friend, Baby James were in the Trackhawk, both of them dripping in designer gear and strapped with Glocks and Mini Draco pistols. The two young men in the backseat were Lil Luke and Baby Lord, two younger members of the Traveling Vice Lords who'd in recent years gained notoriety for their quick tempers and overly active trigger fingers.

The vehicle behind Buck's Trackhawk was a Rolls-Royce Phantom, and it belonged to Markio's much younger cousin Jarvon "Slime" Barnett, a member of the Bloods from the north side of Baton Rouge, Louisiana. His passengers were Dee Dawg, and Baby Joe, childhood friends of his who'd traveled from Baton Rouge to join him in the Windy City. Then came Markio's Rolls-Royce Cullivan. He and Apple, an old friend and fellow TVL he'd known since they were kids on 15th and Trumbull, were in the backseat, Markio working two iPhones while Apple worked on demolishing a jelly-filled Dunkin' donut. Shakia, Markio's youngest sister, sat in the driver's seat talking to their other sister Mariah through her AirPods while a G Herbo track throbbed from the Cullivans' high quality speakers.

Taking up the rear was the second snow-white Trackhawk. Owned by Buck's younger brother, Kay. It too was filled to capacity with heavily armed TVL gang members.

Markio said, "On bro n'em, if we see that nigga Weezy anywhere, I'm hoppin' out myself. That was my muthafuckin' nigga, and he ain't called to tell me shit about this old man tryna get me killed. The fuck kinda shit is that? I had to find out from my lil porn star bitch. If the shoe was on the other foot, I would've called him ASAP."

"You sure you don't want a piece of this donut?" Apple asked, reaching across the armrest with the last bite of donut pinched between his chubby thumb and forefinger. He hardly gave Markio anytime to reply; two seconds later he shrugged his wide shoulders and crammed that oozing bit of donut in his mouth.

Markio paid his old friend Apple no mind. He was ogling a video on Princess Kelly's Onlyfans page on one iPhone while simultaneously using his other iPhone to shop for Bunny on the Louis Vuitton website. He'd seen the anxiety in Bunny's eyes when he forced her to call Big Gabby, and he felt bad for making her feel unsafe in his presence. To make up for it, he was buying her a peacoat, two pairs of sunglasses, five pairs of shoes, and two handbags, obnoxiously pricey items that brought his shopping cart total to $41,874.78. He was ready to complete the purchase but was finding it increasingly difficult to focus on his second phone while on the other phone's screen he had a woman as flawless and bootylicious as Princess Kelly sitting naked at the foot of a king-size canopy bed with her thick legs spread open wide, fucking herself with a large black dildo.

"I can't believe this shit," Markio said, shaking his head and staring at all the creamy white juices that spanned the entire length of the prosthetic penis. "Man do you know how much I love this bad ass bitch? I been wantin' to slide on her for the longest, and Weezy done paid her some bread to set me up?"

"Bunny told you that?" Apple asked.

Markio nodded. "She said Weezy made Princess a Prime Time Girl and gave her that Cuban link she got on in all those new pics and videos she posted to IG this morning, all in exchange for her and her buddy Aqua to set me up for some old school nigga who claim I whacked one of his people."

"You talking about Weezy from Englewood?"

"I damn sure ain't talking about Lil Wayne."

Apple chuckled merrily as he sucked the donut frosting from his fingertips. He was a heavyset brown-skin man in a gray leather Dior jacket over Amiri sweats and Jordan 5 sneakers.

"He might not even follow through on that shit." Apple reasoned. He dried his wet fingertips with a napkin. "You ain't even talked to the nigga yet. Hit him up and see what he got to say about it. Or shit, we can just pop up at Queen of Diamonds tonight. Everybody gon' be there to see Megan Thee Stallion anyway. We can grab a couple VIP tables and slide through with the gang."

"I called Weezy a lil bit ago," Markio said, leaving the Only Fans video to keep himself from becoming aroused in front of Apple. "Some woman answered and said he can't talk right now. I told her to have him hit me back."

Apple started to say something, but Markio's phone began to ring, and when Markio saw that it was Big Gabby calling he held up a forefinger to silence his donut devouring comrade. He answered the FaceTime video call and studied Big Gabby's portly visage. She was snacking on something. *Crunch, Crunch, Crunch.* There were reddish crumbs at the corners of her mouth. Her hair and makeup were done better than a lot of celebrities he'd seen on social media, and her diamond hoop earrings twinkled a rainbow of colors as she returned his furious scowl.

"What's up?" Markio spoke coldly, setting his second phone on the smooth leather armrest so he could focus solely on Big Gabby and whatever it was she had to say.

"Damn," she said, chewing and swallowing. "I can't get a hello. A how you doin'? Is this how you answer your phone nowadays?"

Markio only stared at her. After a couple of seconds, he picked up the Styrofoam cup of Lean from his cupholder and took a generous sip from the cold narcotic beverage. He'd already smoked a dozen blunts of exotic bud and popped a few Percocet pills with the other members of his wealthy young entourage. The drugs dazed him enough to induce distant flashbacks of numerous days and nights he'd spent around Gabby, her family, and the many other residents of Lakeland Projects, a sprawling apartment complex on the north side of Michigan City, Indiana. It was true what they said of him; he'd punched and shot at too many enemies to count in that small town of thirty-two thousand. The thing that a lot of people *didn't* say about him was that he had a lot of love for most of the people he'd met there, loved them the way he loved his own people in Chicago, in fact— and Big Gabby was one of those loved ones.

"What's with this old nigga who been tryna get me out the way?" he asked after a time. "Just tell me his name and we'll be good. No hard feelings at all."

Gabby sucked her teeth indignantly, but she gave him the info he wanted. "His name's Herb. He's an old man who went to war in Vietnam, or somethin' like that. I'd have to ask Weezy the full story. He's in the hospital right now, probably in more pain than either one of us had ever imagined. That old man walked in the club a few hours ago and sliced Weezy's whole hand off. Craziest shit I ever seen in my life."

Markio stuck out his lower lip and nodded his head.

"Listen," said Gabby. "Weezy really on your side. That's the whole reason he lost his hand. The old man tried to get him to have you killed, and it upset Weezy to the point where he reached across the table to strangle him. Herb wants Princess and Aqua to accept a bunch of money to help out with the whole murder scheme, but I don't even think they'll go for it once Weezy tells them the plan. You know Princess is Veemo's baby mama, and Veemo's best friend is your cousin by marriage, right?"

Markio scrunched his brow and shot a glance at Apple. The fat man shrugged once, as if to say, *"Why you lookin' at me?"* And when Markio's gaze returned to the screen of his phone, Gabby said, "You do still fuck with Baby Stone, right? Ain't he some kin to you? Or am I trippin'?"

The name *Baby Stone* made Markio's mouth fall open. It was an involuntary reaction. He tilted his head to one side, silently pandering over the situation with Baby Stone, a gang leader who'd literally gone from friend to foe overnight. It had all started with a 1,500 kilogram shipment of cocaine Markio had received from Mexico's Matamoros drug cartel. He'd fronted four hundred and twenty of those bricks to the one guy he knew could get them sold in a hurry. The man's nickname was Baby Stone. He was a General for a particularly ruthless faction of Black P. Stones in Hyde Park, and if there was one thing Markio knew about Baby Stone, it was that he was practically a genius when it came to dealing drugs.

Markio had heard about Baby Stone several times in the past from some of his fellow gang members who hoped and prayed they would catch Baby Stone slipping one day so they could rob him and make off with some of that money he was always throwing around, and from a couple of bad young hood bitches who'd let him pay four or five hundred for an afternoon of X-rated pleasure— but if not for Markio's aunt Bone, he'd have never met the man in person. Bone's husband and Baby Stone's father were brothers. Bones' husband was a coal-black Vietnam war veteran named Herbert Harris. Markio had never really spoken with Herb;

the old man had come across as quiet and standoffish on the few occasions they'd crossed paths. He always referred to Markio as *"The writer,"* which made Markio feel like there was no shared love between the two of them. Not that Markio needed any love from the elderly fuck. Markio's gang, and the many other gang members and non-gang members he socialized with gave him all the love he needed. Still, Baby Stone was Auntie Bone's nephew through marriage, which made him somewhat of a cousin to Markio. They'd linked up at the Barnett family reunion and agreed to the 420-kilo deal. The following day, Baby Stone's girlfriend had delivered seven large duffle bags full of cash to Markio's friend Tayja's South Loop townhouse, and that same night a box truck full of kilos arrived at Baby Stone's close friend, L Stone's suburban home. Baby Stone paid Markio two million up front, and he'd promised to have the remaining $8.5 million by mid-November. Then, just two weeks ago, Baby Stone had sent Markio a text message: *That $8.5 million over with. Get it how you live."* The message was followed by a demon emoji.

Markio put a million dollars on Baby Stone's head within minutes of reading the message, and his gang had been riding around Hyde Park in Dodge Challenger Hellcats and Jeep Grand Cherokee Trackhawks ever since. They were hopping out every now and then to open fire on the Black P. Stones they'd seen in some of the photos and videos Baby Stone had posted to Instagram. Lil Luke had killed two of them in the past week alone, and Buck had killed another one just yesterday.

With over $120 million stashed away at several different addresses, Markio didn't mind dropping a bag on his opps when he felt it was necessary, He'd paid Lil Luke $100,000 for the double homicide, and even though Buck had his own cash and bricks of coke and heroin, Markio had still paid him $50,000 cash for yesterday's body.

Now, watching Gabby bite down on a stack of hot Doritos, he nodded his head thoughtfully, a triumphant grin slowly raising one side of his mouth.

"I got a bag for you," he said, taking another sip from his cup. "Just tell me where to send it."

"Boy don't nobody want your money," Gabby snapped. "I was calling to tell you what was going on. If anything, I owe you thirty grand. I wouldn't be here if it wasn't for you. Matter fact, where do you want me to send that?"

Markio chuckled once and shook his head dismissively. "Tell Weezy I said to hit me when he get a chance. I know who the old man Herb is. I'm about to get all this figured out now."

He ended the call and sat there in silence for a long moment, replying to text messages on his second iPhone — the prepaid one he'd had registered in a fraudulent name. Every text message he replied to was drug-related. Tayja handled most of the single-digit kilo deals; all of Markio's personal customers bought at least twenty or thirty bricks at a time. Some of them, like Small Body from Indianapolis and Grimey Lord from Milwaukee, had moved up to purchasing one or two hundred bricks of cocaine, heroin, and fentanyl.

"So," Apple asked, "What's the play, Lord?"

Markio answered by addressing his baby sister, who'd braked at the red light and looked at him in the rearview mirror.

"Hillside, Illinois," he said. "Gotta pay my Auntie Bone a quick lil visit.

Chapter 22

The police interview took less time than Princess had expected. After checking her credentials and seeing that she actually did have a valid Concealed Carry License and a valid Firearm Owner's Identification card, they'd recorded her statement of events and let her walk out of the CPD station on 71st Street and Cottage Grove Avenue less than an hour later. She texted Aqua before she even walked out and seen Aqua rushing out of the sliding side door of Day-Day's Mercedes Benz Sprinter van.

"Aaaaagh!" Aqua screamed, wearing a smile that spanned the whole width of her impossibly gorgeous face as she came sprinting at Princess with her arms wide open.

"They got my sis fucked up around this hoe! She done dropped two bodies. The fuuuuuuck!"

Princess laughed and shook her head incredulously as Aqua crossed the parking lot in seven long strides and embraced her in a suffocating hug, jumping up to wrap her legs around Princess's waist and exposing her tongue to do an impromptu twerk on Princess's hip.

"Oh, my God," Princess said smiling, and rolling her eyes. "Let me guess: Day-Day blew a bag to make it up to you, and now y'all back on that lovey-dovey time."

Aqua was nodding happily as she dropped down from Princess hip. She wore a tight pair of black leather pants, a red Gucci skullcap, a puffy red and black Moncler jacket, and red leather knee-high Gucci boots. She held up her left hand to show off the fat yellow diamond on her ring finger.

"He proposed with this two million dollar ring," she said, exposing her tongue again and bouncing her ass to the beat of Offset and Cardi B's *Jealous* as it thumped from the inside of the Sprinter. "Put another $3 million in my bank account before he flew back to Dallas. Aaaand I made him block that trifling hoe Shmoney from all his social media. All that fake bitch got was some dick. I'm the one who really won in the end, so fuck Shmoney and all the rest of them broke hoes she run with."

Princess casted a glance inside the Sprinter. There was a huge bodyguard standing there outside the open passenger's door, but no one else occupied the rear part of the luxury van. All six seats were vacant.

"I told Grind to just drop your car off at my place," Aqua said as the two of them went sauntering toward the van. She lowered her voice to a whisper and added, "I think he and his cousins are going after whoever sent those shooters at him."

"Bunny called me earlier," Princess said, intentionally changing the subject; speaking about Grind and his situation was still a bit of a sore spot. "She told me it ain't all the girls acting like that toward us. Kimmy Kakes and Thick Doll don't have a problem with us being on Prime Shift. It's really just Cherish and Shmoney."

"Figures," Aqua shrugged.

Her long red braids were braided into even thicker braids today. They hung down under the back of her fluffy red skullcap. "Fuck them hoes. If they *want* smoke, we will *give* smoke. Like Peter Gunz said on *Cheaters*, we live in the smoking section. It'll be two more dead bodies around this bitch."

Princess gave another roll of the eyes as she settled into one of the butter-soft leather seats. An episode of *Impact: New York* was playing on the 50-inch television screen that separated the driver's cabin from the rear passenger's compartment. Aqua had a pre-rolled blunt waiting in the ashtray, and Princess wasted no time in lighting it up as the Sprinter van went cruising out of the parking lot and onto Cottage Grove.

Aqua went to her Chase banking app, zoomed in on her checking account balance, and thrust her phone in front of Princess's face. "Just so you can see I ain't cappin," she said.

Princess smirked and nodded as she eyed the account balance: $3,850,000.00.

"Okay, I see you sis," she said, thinking of her own account balance now. She didn't need to pull her banking app to see it. She had exactly $1,132,271.86 in her Chase bank checking account, $1,481,988.64 in her Chase bank savings account, and $125,000 in her extravagant bedroom closet. She taken the $50,000 Weezy had given her and placed it in her wall safe with the other $75,000 in bank new hundreds she kept there in case of emergency.

Aqua snatched her phone back, drummed her thumbs on the screen, and shoved it back in front of her best friend's face. This time Princess found herself looking at a video of Davion Carroll down on one knee, slipping the huge diamond ring onto Aqua's trembling finger as tears cascaded down both of their faces. They were in a classy-looking restaurant with red walls, red tablecloths, and plush red carpeting. Day-Day's bodyguards and several diners stood in the background, observing the proposal with excited smiles and joyful applause. Aqua shouted "Yes!" and leapt into Day-Day's arms the same way she'd just done to Princess outside the police station.

"Aaaaaand he posted it on his IG page," Aqua announced proudly, doing another little dance in her seat. "He done talked to my mama and everything, and I'm flying down there to see him Monday. He wants me to quit dancing and become a homebody. I told him I don't know about all that, but we'll see how he acts."

"As long as he taking care of you financially," Princess said, "And you're willing to forgive him for that dirty shit he did last night, then hey, I'm happy for you."

Princess felt a buzzing inside her purse, so she stuck her hand in the Birkin to find her phone. An anxious look came over Aqua's face as soon as she saw her lifting the iPhone out of her handbag.

"I, uhh," Aqua muttered, averting her eyes and inhaling a mouthful of weed smoke.

Princess squinted, "You *uhh* what?"

"I might've texted Kamari and your mom and told them about that whole shooting thing. Sorry."

Princess's squinted eyelids came even closer to closing completely.

"Bitch, you know I can't hold water!" Aqua exclaimed defensively.

Rolling her eyes in frustration, Princess accepted the blunt from Aqua and took two long pulls on it as she read over her new text messages. He mom accounted for five of the fourteen, and every message was more dramatically urgent than the last. She wanted to know what had happened. She'd seen the double homicide on *Fox* 32's four o'clock news. She'd informed half the family, and now Princess had a vast collection of gang-affiliated uncles and cousins ready to come to her aid. Kamari was just worried. She was already seated in First Class on a Delta flight, flying from Atlanta to Chicago with two of her deceased father's relatives. Grind had sent her a simple two-word message: "Call me." The most unexpected text message of all was the one from Zoodie, the male stripper she'd had a brief fling with in Miami, on the weekend of her 21st birthday. Apparently he was in town and wanted to see if she was available to go out for dinner.

"I hate my life," Princess muttered discontentedly. "Why did Grind have to get out of jail today?"

"Whatever, Pee. I know you're happy he's out. Believe me, I know how whipped that fresh outta jail dick can have a bitch. That's probably what made you shoot those boys who ran up on him."

Princess shook her head. "You don't understand." She showed Aqua the text from Zoodie. "This is the man I was with the night of my 21st B-day. Remember that night? When we stayed the night at that $8,000 a night Palm Island mansion?"

Aqua's lips parted in an audible gasp, and her brow shot up to her hairline. "Him?"

Princess palmed her forehead and moved her head from side to side, slowly and despondently.

"I ain't gon' lie," she said. "Grind got me all the way together in that shower earlier, but Grind ain't Zoodie. That man is a trained professional. He fucked me so good that night, and all day the next day in so many positions. He held me upside down and ate my pussy like that, had blood rushin' to my head while I sucked his dick in a standing 69. He put a gag ball in my mouth so I couldn't scream, tied my wrists to the headboard, and fucked me until I cried. My pussy was sore for two weeks after that. I ain't never been fucked so good in my life."

Aqua's blissful expression morphed into an elated smirk halfway through the panty-drenching story, and as soon as Princess finished talking she held up her finger to show off her ring.

"Didn't you just see Queen Bey this morning?" Aqua asked. "You better take heed to all that game she giving. If Grind liked it then he should've put a ring on it. Until you got one of these on your finger, as far as I'm concerned, you're as single as the last French fry in one of those lil red McDonald's boxes. No salt. No ketchup. No nothin'."

The random analogy sent Princess into a laughing fit that doubled her over and left her gasping for breath. Aqua laughed too. It was a gut-wrenching laughter that relieved

Princess of a lot of the stress she'd felt over the last couple of hours, and when it finally died down, she wiped the tears from her face and shook her head in disbelief.

"You are something else, Aqua. I swear to God. You are a whole damn handful."

"Shiiit." Aqua stared longingly at the multi-million dollar yellow diamond engagement ring on her finger before slipping it off and dropping it into her large red Gucci shoulder bag. "I ain't married yet, either. We might as well go and have us a threesome with that fine ass nigga. That'll be my payback for Day-Day fuckin' Shmoney nasty ass last night."

Princess didn't take long thinking over the plan. She reached forward and high-fived Aqua.

"Let me call this nigga Grind and make sure he ain't fucked up my car," she said. "Then I'ma call my mama and try my best to calm her down before she have our whole family waiting outside my front door."

She FaceTimed Grind, and when the video call began she saw that he had a disturbingly troubled look on his handsome round face like maybe he was under duress. His eyes were focused on something or someone offscreen; he only gave Princess a couple of quick seemingly disinterested glances.

"I just left the police station," she said, her head turned slightly to one side. "They wrote it all up as self-defense. Two of your sister's neighbors let the detectives see the footage from their doorbell cameras. That pretty much cleared me of any wrongdoing."

Grind remained silent. He was looking to his right, listening to a low, sinister voice that sounded somewhat familiar to Princess.

"Uhhmm," Princess said, turning her head a few more degrees to the side, "You have my car, right? Or did you already drop it off at…"

"Nah," Grind interjected, and finally he looked right at her. "It's parked in front of my mama crib on 69th and Lowe."

128

"And you're there with it?"

"Yeah. Don't pull up over this way though. I don't want nobody seeing you with me right now. Grab you a rental or some'n. I'll have my sister drop the car off to you in the morning. It's a whole lotta gang shit goin' on over here, and I don't want you coming nowhere near it. Don't ride through my hood. Don't ride through your hood. Don't even go back to your house in Highland Park. Go over there with Aqua until later tonight. I'll call you later."

Princess gave him a questioning eye, nibbling at one corner of her bottom lip and tapping a roll of ash off the blunt. She said, "Okay, whatever," and ended the video call without another word.

Aqua leaned in. "What? What's wrong?"

"Grind's acting all fucking weird all of a sudden."

"Probably got a bitch over there," Aqua said with a careless shrug. She was already pushing the engagement ring back onto her neatly manicured ring finger. "Fuck that nigga. Hurry up and check on your mama and Vee so we can see what's up with Zoodie."

Chapter 23

Grind pocketed his phone, picked up his Glock, and stood up, leaving his mother's elegantly furnished living room to join the nine other Gangster Disciples who'd gathered around the table in the lemon-scented dining room. Weezy had the floor. He was standing at the head of the table, his right arm heavily bandaged and cradled in a sling, his eyes bloodshot and replete with an intense evil that Grind had never before witnessed in person. Lil D, Smoke G, Mike G, Rose G and Fat Folks were the gang members who'd walked in with Weezy. The other three men were older Jaro City Ganster Disciples, longtime friends of Grind's with whom he'd committed several armed robberies and murders over the years. Their nicknames were Wavy, G-Boy, and Choker. Five of the men toted Dracos and AR pistols with high-capacity drum magazines and tactical lights. All of them wore dark colored ski masks rolled up to their foreheads.

"I don't know who the fuck these niggas think they playin' with," Weezy was saying, "But on Larry Bernard Hoover, somebody gon' die tonight. And we gon' start with them Stones in Hyde Park."

Grind clenched his teeth and squeezed the cold hard butt of his Glock pistol. It too had a drum magazine, one that could hold up to fifty shells. Grind had loaded it with just forty-five hollow tipped rounds to keep it from jamming, and he'd attached a plastic switch to the back of the slide, converting the semi-automatic pistol into a fully automatic machine gun. He knew why Weezy wanted them to go at the Black P. Stones that controlled the poorer sections of the Hyde Park neighborhood. Weezy had just spoken with Millionaire Markio, the famous urban fiction novelist he'd met in prison, and Markio had told him that Baby Stone was ultimately behind the whole plot to extort him into getting Markio killed. It was Baby Stone's uncle, Herb, who'd started calling Weezy from the beginning, and who'd sliced off Weezy's right hand earlier today. Markio's gang of Vice Lords had already started applying pressure to Baby Stone's gang, killing three of them and wounding five more. Now Weezy and his blood thirsty squad of Gangster Disciples were about to turn up the heat, not just on Baby Stone, but Markio as well.

"That nigga Markio told Gabby he was related to Baby Stone." Weezy barked, "So I want y'all to bend some corners through his hood. If you see that white Rolls-Royce truck or that white Phantom, air that muhfucka out. On Larry. And Grind, I want you and Fat Folks to hop out on Princess and whack that bitch too. Do it in front of her crib out there in Highland Park. If you can't catch her there, catch her on her way to the club tonight."

"Why you want us to kill her?" Grind asked defensively. "You know she ain't had no part in this shit."

Weezy was already shaking his head. "Nuh uh. Damn that. All this shit started with Baby Stone and his punk ass uncle, and the one person I know Baby Stone loved like a brother was Veemo, Princess's baby daddy. She gettin' stretched too. Everybody gon' feel my pain. On the GDN."

Grind took a wave brush from his pants pocket and began brushing his hair, something he did when he was bored, or when he was thinking, or when he was feeling particularly upset with someone. He was currently feeling the latter of the three. Weezy went on woofing, barking orders here and there, but Grind tuned it all out and stared at the minute hand on the old grandfather's clock that stood next to his mother's antique China cabinet. The time of day was 5:17 p.m. Mama Rose was around the corner from the house, teaching Bible Studies at St Paul Baptist Church on 70th and Union. She had no idea that her dining room was being used for the devil's work. Had she known, she'd have undoubtedly thrown a fit, cursed them all in the name of Jesus, and beat them upside their heads with the same King James Version of the Holy Bible she was likely preaching from at this very moment.

"And another thing," Weezy spat, walking around the table toward Grind, "The next time I tell you to do some'n, don't question it. You know GD law, lil nigga. I'm the big homie."

The right side of Grind's smooth brown face lifted in a defiant show of aggression. "You're right. I do know law. I know my Sixteen, the I Pledge, the We Pledge, the Coat of Arms, the Blueprint, and a whole lot more. My daddy was a Board Member. It ain't a piece of GD literature that I don't know."

The whites of Weezy's eyes became an even darker shade of red, if that was even possible. Taking another step toward Grind, he pulled a Glock from the waistline of his black Gucci sweatpants. He wore a black Gucci hoodie as well. The hood only covered the back half of his bald head. His pistol had a switch like Grind's, only the magazine was a long 30 shot clip instead of a drum.

"You stickin' outcho chest, lil nigga?" Weezy asked, his tone low and menacing.

Grind shook his head no, his wet lower lip protruding over the upper one, but his unwavering scowl remained.

"I ain't think so. Cause if my memory serves me right, I paid a million dollars to getcho ungrateful ass outta jail. It's time for you to pay that back."

Again, Grind said nothing. His hand tightened around the handle of his pistol, and for two or three seconds he seriously considered raising the handgun from his side and firing a fully automatic burst through the side of Weezy's face. Sure, there would be repercussions, maybe even certain death, but Weezy's head would be knocked halfway off his body, and that was victory enough.

Weezy's breath was hot and pungent on Grind's face. He was 6'9" in height, a full six inches taller than Grind, but no height or weight difference had ever deterred Grind from standing on business. The only factor that kept him from making a brazen attempt on Weezy's life in the middle of his mother's dining room was the knowledge that Princess was now in immediate danger, and he already loved her and her little girl way too much to let anything happen to them. So, instead of lifting his gun he said, "Once this shit over, we clear on that bread, right? I won't owe you nothin'?"

This statement seemed to calm the conflagration behind Weezy's eyes. He gave a subtle nod. "You kill that bitch," he said, "And we're even. You won't owe me a crumb. Matter fact, if y'all kill that bitch, as long as you go to court so I can get the rest of that million dollars back, I'll let you and Fat Folks split whatever the balance is when they send me the check."

Grind's nod was just as subtle. He pocketed his wave brush and reached out for a handshake, and he and Weezy threw up the "rakes", the pitchfork like hand sign that signified their lifelong allegiance to the Gangster Disciple Nation.

"GD Folks!" Lil D shouted and everyone repeated after him.

Three minutes later, they all left Mama Rose's house and piled into a fleet of inconspicuous vehicles that were already half filled with younger gang members who were just as heavily armed and even more eager to jump out on an opp and prove themselves to the guys. Half of the cars and SUVs took off toward Markio's North Lawndale neighborhood, while the others raced off to stalk Baby Stone's gang in Hyde Park.

Grind got in the E-Class Mercedes and drove off, headed for Aqua's Streeterville townhouse, while Fat Folks trailed behind him in a stolen black Buick Envision. He was stopped at a red light, brushing his hair and watching Fat Folks in the rearview mirror, when he started piecing together a plan of action. He hoped like hell it worked.

Chapter 24

There was a six o'clock dress and dance rehearsal scheduled for the dancers who wanted to be a part of Megan Thee Stallion's performance at Queen of Diamonds. The email was sent to everyone on Prime Shift, so Princess and Aqua showed up at exactly 5:35 p.m. They entered through the front doors, draped in diamonds and furs, with three towering Secure Force bodyguards flanking them. A few extra security measures had been put in place since the old man's attack on Weezy. Now there was a metal detector to walk through and also two bouncers with metal detecting wands, and all purses and bags had to be put through an X-ray machine. The additional hassle didn't bother Princess, she'd paid Bee Kay, the bouncer, a hundred dollar bill to carry her purse in through the back door. He handed her the Hermés Birkin as she and Aqua were entering the dressing room area, and she smiled at the considerable weight of it, knowing that her small Glock handgun was concealed inside.

Two of the bodyguards were carrying the designer duffle bags Princess and Aqua had filled with their costumes and other job-related necessities. The email had included a suggestion that the dancers wear purple, so Princess had packed a collection of purple thongs, G-strings, bras, and high-heeled shoes. She and Aqua received a thunderous round of applause from the dancers who were proud that they'd risen through the ranks to become members of the much sought after Prime Shift. Princess smiled and waved. Aqua thanked everyone. Then the two of them continued sauntering through the locker room and into the adjoining health and fitness spa, through there and into the short corridor that led them into the Prime Shift locker room.

There were fourteen other Prime girls in the room, but Princess only eyed the six that mattered: BunnyXXX, Kimmy Kakes, Thick Doll, Sasha the Stallion, Shmoney Rose, and Cherish Taylor. The other girls were background noise, the sort of women who kept to themselves and went with the flow of things. Two of them were white women, two where Hispanic, the other four were black and every single one of them possessed the kind of unmatched beauty and jealousy-inducing curves that could tempt a devoted husband into leaving his family without a second thought.

Bunny, Kimmy, and Thick Doll all smiled when Princess and Aqua entered the room. They got up from the chairs at their makeup tables and rushed over to hug and welcome them into the group. Sasha, Shmoney, and Cherish sat stone-faced at their individual tables casting discreet glances at the newcomers through the reflections of their mirrors, saying nothing. Princess merely grinned and nodded her head.

"I got some 'n for you hoes," she thought to herself as the three friendlier PTG members showed her and Aqua to their new lockers. Princess dismissed the notion of getting away with assaulting Shmoney and Cherish if and when their words came to blows. She was a hundred percent sure that she could beat both of their asses all by herself, and that was exactly what she planned to do if either one of them came at her sideways.

The Secure Force bodyguards set down Princess and Aqua's duffle bags and exited the building. Bunny began telling Aqua all there was to know about Prime Shift, while Kimmy Kakes and Thick Doll helped Princess take everything out of her duffle bag and neatly arrange each item inside her new, much more spacious locker. Princess could almost feel her blood pressure rising higher and higher the more she thought about what Shmoney Rose had done with Aqua's fiancé in the Queen of Diamonds parking lot last night, and the video Cherish Taylor had shared of herself in bed with Small Body this morning. It wasn't that Princess had caught any feelings for the slender young Nap Town trapper; she'd merely wanted to get her rocks off while Grind was in jail. The thing that had Princess so heated was the fact that Cherish had only fucked Body to get under her skin, basically to piggyback off what Shmoney had done with Day-Day. That was what had Princess blood boiling like a pot of overheated tomato sauce.

She glanced back over her shoulder. Cherish, Shmoney, and Sasha were talking amongst themselves, speaking in hushed tones. The other eight Prime Time Girls were seated on a huge U-shaped sofa, a few of them adjusting their costumes, several others lost in the screens of their smartphones, all of them discussing the shocking sword attack Weezy had suffered earlier in that day. A City Girls music video was playing on the massive wall mounted television. Three bottles of Casamigos stood half empty on the cocktail table in the middle of the spacious square room. There was a large restroom in the back, and Princess couldn't hold back the conspiratorial grin that formed at the corners of her pretty mouth as she considered all the felonious assaults she could get away with in that restroom where there were no cameras to catch her in action.

Princess was opening the box to her new combination lock when the pressure of being in the same room with Cherish Taylor got the best of her. She turned to face the room, her cute brown visage twisting into a venomous scowl, her impeccably manicured fingers moving low to grab hold of her hips. Glowering at Cherish, she made a noisy show of clearing her throat, and as soon as Cherish looked her way she set in.

"Bitch, if you got a problem, we can go right in that restroom over there and handle it. You too, Shmoney. Y'all honestly think I give a fuck about somebody fucking a man I met last night? Small Body broke bread and got a lap dance, and that's probably the last time I'll ever see him. And as for Shmoney and Day-Day fuckin' out there in the parking lot like some homeless bums, I really could care less about that either. But I'll tell you what."

Princess slipped he hand down into the Birkin bag she had hanging down from her shoulder, closing her fingers around the butt of her pistol. She took two steps in Shmoney Rose's direction and smirked when Shmoney flinched to the side.

"If one of y'all come for my sis, Aqua again," Princess continued, "I'm taking it like you're coming for me personally. I done already got away with dropping two bodies today. I ain't got no problem trying for another two."

Cherish rose slowly from her chair. She was a stunningly attractive, big booty Brazilian-American woman with full lips, high cheekbones, and a smoothly unblemished reddish-brown complexion. She wore skintight purple booty shorts and a purple lace bra that was transparent enough to expose the entirety of her D-cup melons. Her purple leather knee-high YSL boots had seven inch heels and spaghetti strings tied all around them. Her Cuban link necklace was almost as thick as the ones Princess and Aqua wore, and she had a "bussdown" Cartier watch on her left wrist that dripped in VVS diamonds.

Taking it like Cherish was standing up to her, Princess tightened her grip on the Glock in her purse. She was almost tempted to pull it out and take aim, but then Cherish surprised her.

"I apologize," Cherish said. "I was on bullshit, I can't lie, but it was only because Weezy bought you and Aqua bigger chains than the ones he bought us. That shit made me jealous."

Sasha stood up behind Cherish and nodded her head in agreement. Shmoney Rose was the next one to stand. The two of them lowered their heads in cowardice, both pretending to be engrossed in social media on their iPhone.

"Damn," Kimmy Kakes said as she walked up beside Princess. "I heard that was you who shot those boys over there on Hermitage. I thought it was a rumor. They say it was MCG and Snake, two of the Mickey Cobras."

"It ain't no fuckin' rumor," Princess said, unable to keep herself from glowering at Cherish. "I'm with all the bullshit, and my people got seven tables out there. Three in VIP and four more right outside the locker room door. We almost thirty deep in this hoe, and we'll tear the club up on whoever wanna turn up."

Princess had a few more threatening words to voice, but Big Gabby entered the room at that very moment. She had a clipboard in one hand. A petite bronze-skinned woman in dark purple leggings and a matching sports bra followed Gabby into the room. The woman had curly brown hair and freckles, full juicy lips and intelligent gray eyes. She seemed to sense tension in the room as soon as she got a whiff of the air, immediately flicking her eyes from Princess to Cherish and Shmoney.

"Okay," Gabby began, "this lovely young woman I have with me is Lauren McQueen. She'll be your choreographer for the whole Megan Thee Stallion show. It'll be a thirty minute set, and after that I need all of PTG in the VIP lounge. Every celebrity in the city will be up there with stacks of dollars piled over their heads. I won't name them all, but Alexus and Bulletface will be in the building, so you know what kind of night this could end up being. MBM might throw four or five hundred grand in the air. Maybe even more than that."

Kimmy raised her hand. "Where are we supposed to be practicing these dance moves?"

"Third floor training room. Get there."

The girls, many of them jittery with excitement, began trailing the curly-haired choreographer out of the room. Reluctantly, Princess secured her locker and joined the outgoing line of gorgeous young women. She was just as eager to showcase her talents in front of H-Town's number one hot girl, but Big Gabby reached out and took hold of her elbow before she could reach the door. Aqua stopped too.

"Wait a second. I need to talk to you and Aqua in my office."

Princess rolled her eyes in dramatic fashion. "We got the money for the fine. I'll bring it when we tip in later on tonight," she said, grabbing her hip again.

Gabby shook her head. "No. It ain't about that. It's about Weezy, and trust me, it's something you both need to hear."

Aqua turned to look up at Princess, uncertainty lifting her brow an inch. She wore a purple Gucci print catsuit over violet colored Christian Louboutin heels, and she looked absolutely stunning. After a second, she shrugged her shoulders and left out behind Big Gabby. Princess sighed out loud, rolled her eyes, and hung the strap of her Birkin purse from her shoulder as she and Aqua strolled next door to Big Gabby's office. She thought of the two young men she'd shot through the face on 60th and Hermitage as she stepped into Gabby's office. Their names were Donte Edgebrook and Keytron Douglas, 31 and 27, respectively, and according to the Chicago Police Department street gang database, both Donte and Keytron were members of the Gutterville Mickey Cobras. Princess knew of them. She'd spent all her formative years in and around the Hyde Park neighborhood, so she was familiar with all the street gangs, from Baby Stone's gang of Black P Stones to the Gutterville Mickey Cobras, the Fifth Ward, and New Town Black Disciples, the Row Row Gangster Disciples, and the Hobos. Dozens upon dozens of seemingly heartless black men who lived and died by the gun, the kind of men who sold drugs, robbed other dope boys for drugs and jewelry, extorted legitimate business owners, taunted other gangs with disrespectful hand signs, and habitually emerged from lightning fast sports cars with masks on their heads and pistols in hand to chase down and murder their enemies. Princess made a couple of phone calls while she and Aqua were packing their bags. Her Hyde Park people had come through for her like they always had, arriving at Queen of Diamonds before she'd ever climbed back into the Mercedes Sprinter van to head back to the club. They'd smiled pridefully from their tables and used their smartphones to stream live video of Princess walking into the club, but she hadn't taken the time to acknowledge them. She'd been far too deep in her feelings about Cherish and Shmoney as she was now.

She came back to the present when she watched Big Gabby plop down in the swivel chair behind her desk. Gabby's fleshy cheeks swelled as she put on one of her rare smiles. She typed at her computer for a couple of seconds, licked her glossy lips and crushed an empty bag of Flamin' Hot Doritos into a ball before tossing it into the trash can next to her closed restroom door.

"First of all," Gabby said, "I'd like to say I'm really proud of you for standing up to Cherish the way you just did. Lauren and I sat here and listened to the whole thing, watched it all on camera. You reached in that Birkin like you had a gun or something."

Princess inhaled sharply and looked at Gabby with wide eyes. "No, uhh," she said, thinking up an excuse. "I just have a habit of reaching in my purse when I'm arguing. That's usually where I keep my gun, but of course I don't have it on me now."

Gabby waved it off. "Cherish needed to be checked. She always bossing the other hoes around. It's refreshing to see somebody who doesn't back down from her."

Aqua laughed. "I'm sorry, but this is Princess we're talking about here. This bitch ain't backing down from nobody."

Princess folded her arms across her chest and stuck one foot back to gently kick the office door shut behind her. She felt her iPhone vibrating in her purse. Glancing down, she found that her Hermés bag was open just wide enough to see the incoming call on her phone screen. It was her daughter's father, Veemo, calling from Menard Correctional Center. His cellmate, Marcus White, had bribed a prison guard into smuggling in a cell phone two days ago. Veemo had called once already to speak with Princess and their daughter without his call being monitored He rarely ever called Princess more than once every couple of weeks, so she was pretty sure his reason for calling again had something to do with her shooting the two Mickey Cobras who'd tried to run down on her new man.

"No disrespect, Big Gabby," Princess said digging the phone out of her purse. "But I have an important phone call coming in right now, and we need to be getting upstairs to that audition. Can you hurry up and tell us what's up?"

She answered the call, told Veemo to hold on a second, and looked at Gabby waiting for an explanation.

Gabby's rare smile spread another inch, officially making it the broadest smile Princess had ever seen on her.

"Weezy and Millionaire Markio spoke on the phone," Gabby said.

She twisted the cap off a tall plastic bottle of Dr. Pepper soda and drank down five or six ounces of it.

"They were able to piece this whole thing together. Baby Stone owes Markio somewhere around eight million dollars, and instead of paying up front he told Markio to *get paid.* That might not have been the smartest move. Markio put a million dollars on Baby Stone's head and sent some shooters at his gang. That's what made Baby Stone and his Uncle Herb try to extort Weezy into getting you and Aqua to set Markio up so they could get him killed."

Aqua gasped and turned to gawk at Princess. She was clearly thinking what Princess was thinking. Over the past

142

week, several of the boys and three of the girls in Princess's old neighborhood had been chased down and shot by a crew of unknown masked gunmen. Three of those boys had died. One of them was Braylen Dobbs, the sixteen-year-old brother of Princess's childhood friend, Nishelle Dobbs. Braylen's older brother Braylon was among the men who now sat alongside Baby Stone's close friend L-Stone and eleven Black P. Stones in the VIP lounge.

So, Millionaire Markio was responsible for Braylen's murder?

This was shocking news to Princess. She'd been a fan of his books ever since the release of his first hit novel. He was an exceedingly talented African American urban fiction writer who appeared humble and respectable in all of his Facebook posts, but she'd heard rumors of his reputation in the streets. If he and Baby Stone were indeed at odds, then Baby Stone and his gang were in serious trouble.

"Is that why we were switched to Prime Shift?" Aqua asked.

Big Gabby nodded her head. "The old man Herb pretty much demanded it. Makes sense now, though. Baby Stone and Veemo were like brothers, and Veemo has a daughter by Princess. I can see Baby Stone trying to get the two of you to move to Prime. He has a kid with Thick Doll, so I'm sure he knows about all the money our Prime Shift girls make on a nightly basis. He probably did it to look out for Veemo."

Princess furrowed her brow and folded her arms over her chest, holding her phone in her hand. She sincerely hoped Veemo was listening to everything Gabby was saying.

"Anyway," Gabby went on. "I called you two in here for one reason and one reason only. You may not like what I have to say, but trust me, it's for the best."

"Okay, okay," Princess said impatiently. "Just tell me."

"I don't think it's safe for y'all to be her tonight." Gabby said, rotating in her chair to look back at her closed restroom door just as someone flushed the toilet beyond it. She quickly spun back to lock eyes with Princess. "Weezy is pissed the fuck off right now. I wouldn't be surprised if he sends somebody after you over this whole thing with Baby Stone. He might've already paid somebody to do it for him. You do know it was Weezy who paid Grind's bond, don't you? He sent me to deliver the check and do the paperwork. That was all his money. Have you asked Grind what he owes Weezy for those million dollars?"

Princess squinted and tilted her head to one side as the idea that Grind might be plotting against her slowly began to register in her brain. She snatched a glance at her phone screen and was glad to see that the call had not ended. Veemo was still on the line listening, listening, listening.

"I honestly think your lives are in jeopardy if y'all stay here to perform tonight." Gabby pressed on. "Book a flight to some exotic island and treat yourselves for a few days. Give all this negative energy some time to pass. Shit, Aqua, you just got engaged to Davion Carroll. His net worth is $345 million. What are you even doing here? You've won."

Aqua rolled her eyes and smiled like a fool, holding up her hand to show off the engagement ring. With her icy Cuban link necklace and diamond Cartier watch, she could easily have been mistaken for a member of YoungNya's Plush Gang crew. She was a multimillionaire stripper from the burbs, a bad little yellow bone with a perfect round ass, a remarkably cute face, and a bubbly naïve personality that made all the men feel like they could snag her if they were afforded a chance.

On the other hand, the only thing bubbly about Princess was her huge bubble butt, and she was far from naïve. She took one cordless Apple earbud from inside her purse and stuck it in her left ear. Gabby watched her with close scrutiny, probably wondering who was listening on the other end of the phone line. Then Princess did something that made Big Gabby's scrutinizing eyes widen with concern.

She pulled the Glock pistol from inside her purse and pointed the barrel at Gabby's buxom chest.

Aqua gasped. "Girl, what the hell…?"

"Who's in that restroom over there?" Princess asked. She spoke in a low, controlled tone of voice, her gaze flicking right and left from the restroom door to Gabby and back again.

"What are you talking about?" Gabby asked incredulously. "And how did you get that gun in here?"

"You just told me I might be in danger if I stay here and work tonight," Princess said. "Then, out of nowhere, the toilet in your restroom flushes, and nobody comes out. Who's in there?"

Slowly Big Gabby rolled back in her chair and rose to her bare feet. Apparently she kicked off her designer heels somewhere under the desk. She walked to the closed restroom door, turned the knob, and pulled it open. Princess swung her pistol to aim into the restroom just as a tall, dark-skinned, bald headed man in a dark blue sweatshirt and jeans appeared in the doorway. She recognized him immediately and dropped the pistol back into her purse before he could get a glimpse of it. The man was Tyrone Steele. Princess had watched him in action too many times to count. He was perhaps the most well-endowed man in the adult film industry. Seeing him in person made Princess's jaw drop. He closed one arm around Gabby's waist and brought her close, kissing her on the cheek. He shifted his smoldering gaze to Princess and Aqua.

Big gabby said, "This my new friend Tyrone…"

"We know exactly who he is," Aqua cut in. "The question is what is he doing here? How did you meet him?"

The concern in Gabby's eyes vanished in an instant. She placed the palm of her hand flat on the muscular chest of Tyrone's fitted Burberry sweater, eased it down to the shockingly notable bulge in the front of his jeans, and spent a long moment rubbing and caressing the serpentine print of his intimidating, lengthy penis.

"He and I have a bit of an arrangement," Gabby said, beaming a ten thousand watt smile that put all of her Colgate white veneers on full display. "As a matter of fact, you two can head on up to that audition. Tell the other girls I'll be busy for the next hour or so, and I don't want any interruptions. Princess, you and I will talk later."

Princess smirked. Turning to leave, she could hear both Veemo and Baby Stone speaking in her ear, so she knew that Veemo had likely phoned Baby Stone on three-way sometime during the call.

"Thank you so much, Prinny," Baby Stone was saying. "That's all I needed to hear."

Chapter 25

Tyrone Steele practically salivated as he watched the two young women saunter out of Big Gabby's office. Both women were beyond stunning. Ogling the jaw dropping curves on the slightly taller, darker skinned stripper aroused Tyrone even more than the feel of Gabby's hand on his rapidly hardening dick. He tilted his head downward to lock eyes with Gabby as soon as her office door swung shut. He kissed her on the mouth while slipping his arms around her waist, and he sank his hands into the flesh of her fat bouncy ass, smacking and squeezing while repeatedly planting kisses on her thick, juicy lips.

It was the text message he'd received from BunnyXXX that had landed him here at Queen of Diamonds in the first place.

"I know this might sound crazy, but the house mom at the strip club I dance at say she got a bag for you to come through and dick her down. She's a big girl, but she's sexy, and rich."

"How much $$ are we talking?" Tyrone replied.

"Idk. Just call and talk to her."

Bunny had messaged him Gabby's phone number, and Tyrone had called her right away. It had taken less than a minute for them to get to the cash offer. $10,000 for a single night, or $50,000 for the entire weekend. Tyrone had wisely opted for the $50,000 cash offer. He already had a thing for BBWs. His ex-wife Shyanne was a heavyset woman, and he'd enjoyed fucking her nearly every day for more than seven years. The cash Gabby was paying him was really just an added bonus, because he'd dick her down for free.

Big Gabby was well over 250 pounds, but he picked her up with no trouble at all and carried her to her desk. As soon as her ass landed on the smooth wooden surface, he pushed up her dress and went to his knees in front of her, first inhaling the honey sweet fragrance of her vagina and then moving in for a taste. She tasted even sweeter than she smelled. He shoved her ankles high in the air, and she fell back on her hands. He dipped a middle finger into her warm, tight little pussy hole and hungrily licked his lips when her plentiful juices trickled down the sides of his probing finger. Flickering his tongue across her engorged clitoris, he flared his nostrils and inhaled again. To Tyrone Steele, there was nothing in the world that smelled more scrumptious than a black woman's pussy.

He licked and sucked on Gabby's clitoris until his dick became painfully hard in his jeans. Then he stood and undid his belt, grinning at Gabby as her focus descended to his impressive bulge. He unbuttoned the jeans, pushed them down to his fresh white Nike sneakers, and stepped out of them. Big Gabby's mouth fell open, and she started fingering herself as Tyrone began stroking his huge snake of a penis. He smacked his fat black cockhead against her glistening wet labia while he contemplated going in his pocket to dig out the extra-large Magnum condoms he'd brought along with him.

As if reading his mind, Big Gabby said, "I got my tubes tied five years ago, and I ain't had no dick in 6 months. I visit my OB\GYN once a month. Never had an STD in my life. You can shoot the club up for all I care."

Tyrone chuckled merrily. He was well aware of the younger generation's lingo. Shooting the club up was another way of saying he could penetrate her without using protection and ejaculate inside her pussy. In the porn world, it was called a vaginal cream pie. Tyrone was eager to feel Gabby's slippery vaginal walls gripping the length of his dick. So, he pressed the head into that snug little hole of hers and watched her eyes bulge as he moved forward, skewering the big woman on what was undoubtedly the largest erect penis she'd ever had in her. Her vaginal walls flexed and stretched around the considerable girth of his thick, black erection. It was a tight fit. He held her thick brown legs back and stared down into her wide eyes as he began sliding his massive organ in and out of her. He kissed her on the mouth, his parted lips connected with hers, and for a while he allowed passion to take the wheel, gradually increasing the speed and depth of his thrusts until he established a deeply penetrating rhythm that made it impossible for Gabby to close her incessantly moaning mouth.

As he fucked her, Tyrone found it easy to push one particularly troubling image to the back of his mind. It was the daunting memory of the gun he'd seen pointed in his direction when he first exited the restroom a few minutes earlier. He'd played it cool, keeping his eyes on Gabby, but he'd seen it just the same. The white diamond pendant perched between the armed woman's perky boobs had read Princess, and she'd worn a disturbing frigid expression that left very little doubt as to whether she'd fire her pistol at the slightest hint of threat.

Tyrone had a gut feeling that the gun toting exotic dancer was a truly dangerous woman like Pam Grier in all those black gangster flicks he'd watched with his uncles as a kid. Oddly enough, the indelible memory of Princess pointing her gun at him turned Tyrone on, and for a short time he imagined that it was her sitting on the desk in front of him. He moved close to Big Gabby, pressed his fingers into the fatty flesh of her thighs, and fucked her like he was trying to make a baby.

Chapter 26

"You need to get out of that club," Veemo said in Princess's ear.

She and Aqua had left Big Gabby's office only to pause and linger near the three vending machines ten feet away. Aqua stood with her hands resting on her hips, looking up at Princess. She had one of the AirPods in her ear, listening in on the conversation Princess was having with Veemo and Baby Stone.

"I ain't going nowhere," Princess replied. "There is money to be made, and I'm about to make it."

"Benny Moe and his nephew just got hit up on 51st," Baby Stone said. "Some niggas pulled up on the side of his BMW and hung out the windows with Glocks and Dracos. Aired 'em out. Killed both of 'em. That's five of the Moes we done lost in the past three days. This shit done got too serious, Prinny. Fall back and let us take care of these fuck niggas."

Princess responded with an indignant suck of her teeth and folded her arms across her chest. "Nuh uh." She shook her head no. "I'm raking it up tonight. There are about to be as many pro athletes and rich street niggas in here to see Meg. I know at least eight of my followers who's already posted that they'll be in the building, and they're all millionaires."

"We don't need their money," Aqua muttered vacantly. "I just showed you how much bread I got from that nigga Day-Day. I think we should listen to Big Gabby. We could just go somewhere. We can take Vee with us and spend a week or two at Day-Day's mansion in Houston."

"Listen to your girl," Veemo said. "Aqua get her outta there."

"L-Stone got the gang in this bitch with us," Princess pointed out. "They're on the main floor *and* in VIP. Let Weezy and his boys try some shit if they want to. We'll send this bitch up."

Veemo started to argue his point, so Princess ended the call right then, rudely and abruptly. She'd never had much patience with Veemo, especially when he was telling her what to do. She viewed herself as a boss. If her own parents couldn't dictate her actions, she certainly wasn't about to let some incarcerated man do it.

She snatched her AirPod from Aqua's ear and dropped it in her purse, and for the next couple of seconds she and Aqua stared silently at one another, Aqua holding her own phone in one hand and trying desperately not to look down at the engagement video she had playing on the screen; Princess chewing at the inside of her cheek as she considered Baby Stones's sneakily secret move to get her placed on Prime Shift amid his turmoil with Weezy and Millionaire Markio.

Finally, Aqua glanced down at the video. Princess looked at it too, first regarding the heartwarming video with mild disinterest, then narrowing her eyes and moving in for a closer look when she spotted something of interest in the background. Just as Day-Day was kneeling in front of Aqua and digging in the jewelry box from his pants pocket, and old, coal black man who was seated three tables back turned to see what the excitement was about. Then the younger, brown-skinned man seated directly across from the old man turned around to look back at the captivating proposal. The brown skinned young man was Baby Stone, and it took Princess's exceptionally intelligent brain less than one second to figure out that old man's identity. He was Herbert Harris, the very same old man who'd walked into Queen of

Diamonds and left Weezy with a bleeding stump at the end of his powerfully muscled right arm.

"That's him," Princess said, in whispering tones of astonishment. "That's the old man who cut Weezy's hand off."

She pointed an index finger at the wrinkly face old man. He looked older than Morgan Freeman. Aqua tilted her head to the side and knitted her brow like a curious kitten. She restarted the video and zoomed in on the old man's table, and as she did, Princess saw two other men she'd known for years, Mike Mo and L-Stone. They were seated at the nearby table with two younger women.

"It was Baby Stone who put us all in this bullshit, and now he wants us to go running when the shit hits the fan," Princess said in disbelief. "His goal from the very beginning was to get us to set up Millionaire Markio, all because he owed Markio some money and didn't wanna pay."

"Well, that was a pretty stupid plan," said Aqua. "There's no way in hell he could've got us to set up Markio."

And she was right. Both Princess and Aqua were avid readers of urban fiction novels, and Millionaire Markio was by far their favorite author of all time. He was a modern day Donald Goines, a literary prodigy with the God-given wits to vividly depict the many highs and lows of the Black American experience.

Back in February, Princess had taken Aqua to one of Markio's book signings. They'd purchased signed copies of his number one bestselling The Bird Man book series, the thrilling urban saga that had recently been turned into a movie starring several A-list actors including Creed star Michael B. Jordan and the incomparable Taraji P. Henson. Princess had screamed with joy the next day when she checked Markio's Instagram page and saw that he had followed her back. She'd FaceTimed Aqua to share the news, only to learn that he had followed her too. The next day, during a weekend stay in The Bahamas, they'd posted photos of themselves reclined in lounge chairs outside a Paradise Island resort, reading their signed copies of Markio's books and to this day Princess could still remember the jittery feeling she'd experienced when she discovered that Markio had liked the photos and shared them to his own Instagram page.

Princess shook her head and exhaled a sigh of frustration. Her phone rang with a FaceTime call from her sister Kamari just as Aqua asked, "So, what are we gonna do?"

Princess shrugged and held up a forefinger as she answered the video call.

"Big sis!" Kamari said excitedly. "Where are you right now? Are you in the club? Because I just pulled into the parking lot, and I don't see your car anywhere."

Kamari's complexion was darker than Princess's. She too wore a diamond encrusted Cuban link necklace, only instead of her name the pendant read *PLUS GANG* in large white diamond lettering. Her Louis Vuitton bucket hat matched her leather bubble jacket. She was a jaw dropping paragon of African American beauty, and thanks to her deceased father's rap star wife, YoungNya and his billionaire sister Johnna Broward, Kamari was a rising star in the black community.

"Grind's supposed to be dropping my car off at Aqua's place," Princess said and suddenly she became thoughtful, squinting her eyes and wondering if Weezy had paid Grind's bond in exchange for one deadly favor.

"We, uhh.. came in that black Sprinter van."

"Come out here," Kamari said. "I know you're probably busy as fuck right now, but trust me, I have some really good news."

"What kind of good news? Because I'm supposed to be upstairs rehearsing for…"

"Just come outside. I'm in the black Escalade."

Princess rolled her eyes and ended the video call. She looked at Aqua. "Let's run outside real quick. Then we can go up there and see what's to that dance routine."

After returning to their new locker room to retrieve their furs, Princess and Aqua walked hurriedly toward the rear exit door. A single bouncer sat in the small room to the left of the door, chowing down on a serving of hot wings while eyeing the Panneton cameras on the widescreen television monitor in front of him. He offered to escort them outside and Aqua politely declined, her Secure Force bodyguards had been waiting in the Sprinter van, and she'd already messaged them saying she and Princess were on their way out.

Princess caught a fleeting glimpse of five white vehicles entering the parking lot on the bouncer's TV monitor, but she didn't think anything of it until she pushed the door open and stepped out into the cold. The detail that really grabbed her attention was the front of the leading vehicle. It was a Bugatti Veyron. The next two vehicles were Rolls-Royces, a Cullivan and a Phantom. The last two were Jeep Cherokee Trackhawks. Kamari's matte black Cadillac Escalade ESV was idling right beside Aqua's Mercedes Sprinter van. And there were two white Chevy Suburbans idling to the left of it. Walking toward the Escalade, Princess stared into the Bugatti's windshield until she identified the driver. When she saw who it was, she gasped and grabbed hold of Aqua's elbow. They kept walking, but Aqua instantly turned to see what had snatched her bestie's attention, and when she saw him she gasped too.

Millionaire Markio was driving the Bugatti. Light skinned and notably handsome, he seemed to be staring right at Princess and Aqua. Sure, he had a pair of Cartier sunglasses over his eyes, but they weren't dark enough to conceal the direction of his unwavering gaze.

Kamari pushed open the Escalade's rear passenger side door and jumped out with a huge smile on her beautiful chocolate face. She hugged Princess, hugged Aqua, and then threw her hand back to scream at the cool blue skies above.

"You're not gonna believe this!" Kamari said, jumping up and down with excitement. "I told Nya about the whole shooting situation what went down earlier, and about you being switched to Prime Shift. She spoke with Alexus about it, and they came up with a great idea!"

Princess squinted thoughtfully. She was more than interested. Alexus Costilla was the multi-billionaire CEO of Costilla Corporation, which owned the Minority Television Network, MTN Studios, and a hundred other Fortune 500 companies. Alexus was married to Blake "Bulletface" King, the billionaire CEO of Money Bagz Management, one of the top five Hip Hop record labels in the music industry. He signed Nya to MBM earlier this year.

Aqua sucked her teeth. "Kamari, will you get to the point? We got things to do."

Rolling her pretty brown eyes as Millionaire Markio seven figure sports car pulled up behind the Suburbans, Kamari said, "It's a TV show big, sis. *The Real Bad Bitches of Chicago*. It'll air on MTN and stream on the MTN app. Alexus said she'll make you an executive producer. She's basically putting you in position to be the next Shaunie O'Neal, only instead of Basketball Wives, your show will be all about the Prime Time Girls here at Queen of Diamonds, and you'll have complete creative control over the project."

Princess eyelids widened almost instantly, and a surprised smirk raised the corner of her mouth. She put her hand on her hips and was imagining herself as a reality TV star when Markio pushed open his door and climbed out. The doors to the four vehicles that had trailed him swung open almost simultaneously, and his boys emerged looking like rich young gangsters.

Markio gave Princess and Aqua a hint of a nod. He was chewing gum, holding a double stacked Styrofoam cup with a neatly drawn five pointed star scrawled on the side in red ink. The letters L, T, P, F and J were written outside the points of the star. Princess guessed his entire outfit had cost him at least fifteen grand. His jewelry: $500,000 easily. He walked to the Suburban that was parked alongside Kamari's Escalade and disappeared behind its driver's side. The other boys stood watch beside their whips, their eyes darting left and right, smoke from their blunts billowing into the cool winter air.

"I'm with it," Princess said, after a time. "Tell her I'm with it."

"You can tell her yourself," Kamari said,

At first, Princess figured Kamari was about to raise her phone to FaceTime Alexus, the woman who, according to Forbes, was the world's wealthiest living person. Instead, Kamari spun around and peered toward the two Surburbans. Three seconds later, the doors of both Surburbans were opened and a brown skinned woman in a full length white fur coat was helped out of the rear driver's side door Markio was standing next to. Even from twelve feet away Princess could clearly discern the woman's unprecedented beauty. Markio walked next to her as eight brawny Hispanic men accompanied them toward Princess, Aqua, and Kamari.

Princess's eyes lit up. She tried to swallow and found it impossible. Her heart seemed to have risen into her throat, effectively blocking off her airway. She was a huge fan of Markio's work, but there were only two people on earth with enough star power to make Princess completely forget about her audition for tonight's celebrity performance, and one of them was Alexus Costilla.

"Hello. Nice to meet you," Alexus said, her glossy lipped smile revealing two rows of perfect, white teeth. She embraced Princess in a welcoming hug, did the same to Aqua, and then motioned toward Markio as he took a swig from his cup. "This here's a close friend of mine. I believe there's some sort of misunderstanding between him and a friend of yours, and since Markio and I are currently working together on several film projects, I believe it's my best interest to mediate the situation."

Alexus swept her eyes around the parking lot, as if searching for a place to do such mediating. Her long waterfall of hair was jet black, her eyes a warm emerald green, and her sharply pointed fingernails were painted white, matching her fur coat and Yves Saint Laurent boots.

"Let's not do it here," she said finally, "I understand you two work here, so I'm willing to compensate you for your time. How does a million dollars apiece sound?"

Aqua spoke first: "Shit, where we goin'?"

Princess snickered, rolling her eyes, and shaking her head. She had to admit, though. A million dollars was one hell of an offer.

"Let us grab our bags," she said, flicking a second glance at Millionaire Markio. "We can go to my place. Kamari and I own a house in Highland Park."

"Sounds like a plan," Alexus said with a nod. She turned and walked back to her SUV; the eight large Mexican men all of them wearing identical white Gucci peacoats and white leather boots, moved alongside her like specially trained military veterans.

Princess was walking back toward QOD's rear exit door when she received an alert from her Panneton home security cameras. She checked her phone and saw that a dark colored Buick SUV had just parked in front of her Highland Park estate. She eyed it suspiciously, thinking of Weezy and the money he'd spent to bond Grind out of jail, and Big Gabby's ominous warning that Grind might owe Weezy for the favor.

Zooming in on the SUV, Princess stared through its passenger's side window. She couldn't see the passenger's head, but what she could see on the camera's high resolution video was the passenger's dark blue designer jogging suit, and the bulky black pistol he had on his lap. It was Grind, and as far as Princess was concerned, there was only one reason he'd be parked in front of her house with a gun on his lap.

Next to the rear exit door was an intercom button. Aqua pressed it. The camera above the door panned, tilted, and zoomed, and then the bouncer buzzed them in.

"That Bugatti still got the paper tag on it," Aqua noted. "He must've bought it recently."

Princess didn't comment on the matter, but she did look back at Markio as he settled into the driver's seat of his brand new Bugatti Veyron. He was watching her with an intrigued smirk on his handsome brown face.

Back in the locker room, she repacked her things in a hurry. Aqua had the Secure Force bodyguards come in to help them carry their bags out to the Sprinter, and by then Princess had made a decision on what to do about Grind.

Chapter 27

Grind lit a Newport cigarette and sat back in his seat, listening to Wooski's *Computers* as it throbbed from the Buick's speakers and strolling through Instagram on his iPhone while Fat Folks rocked back and forth in the driver's seat.

"Folks, you heard what that nigga Weezy said?" Fat Folks exclaimed. His eyes gleamed with joy. "He gon' let us split a whole fuckin' million! Nigga, I'm trickin' all that shit off. On the G. I'ma grab me a whip, crib, and some clothes, and the rest of that shit getting tricked off on bad bitches. I want that bad ass porn star who dance at Queen of Diamonds. What's her name again? Bunny? On fo'nem, I'll pay that bitch twenty bands to sit on my face."

Grind turned to Fat Folks and regarded him with an expression of supreme dislike. He hated lames with a passion, and Fat Folks was one of the lamest niggas he'd ever met. Puffing on his cigarette, he raised the volume on the Wooski song and stared out his window at the most beautiful home on the street. There was an eight foot redbrick wall surrounding the property and a ten foot wrought iron gate that opened into a concrete walkway leading through the front lawn and up to the front door. A pair of wrought iron gates opened into the huge cobblestone driveway. There were cameras mounted on top of the redbrick walls, above the gates, and every exterior corner of the obnoxiously spacious Highland Park mansion.

"I might grab a couple of bows of some exotic shit to smoke on," Fat Folks continued, "But I ain't doin' no hustlin' That half a ticket gon' last me the rest of my life, watch. I'm have all the hoes. On fo'nem grave."

Grind sucked his teeth and glared at Fat Folks. "You's a stupid ass nigga," he said, and left it at that.

"Whatever," Fat Folks shot back. "You just make sure you don't freeze up when it's time to whack that bitch."

Fat Folks pulled a Pooh Shiesty mask down over his head and reclined in his seat. His chubby, light brown fingers were wrapped around an AR pistol. He wore a black Reebok hoodie that might have been ten years old, threadbare black sweatpants, and an old pair of horribly wrinkled Timberland boots. He smelled the way he looked: dirty, rotten, and musty. Even his dreadlocks possessed a sickening stench.

Grind slipped his forefinger in over his Glock's double trigger and clenched his teeth. He took several calming breaths that didn't at all help to settle his frayed nerves. He searched QOD on Instagram and resisted the urge to react to the photo of Princess and Aqua he saw when he found the page. Whoever ran the page had posted the revealing photo to announce that the two of them had officially became Prime Shift Girls. Their faces were also advertised on the flyers announcing Megan Thee Stallion's special performance. He was still studying the photos when his phone rang with a call from Princess. He stopped breathing and stared at her contact photo. It showed her standing in her walk-in closet, smiling from ear to ear as she held her joyously laughing daughter in the air.

Fat Folks sat up and looked at Grind's phone. "That's that bitch right there," he said. "The fuck you waitin' on? Answer the call, nigga!"

Reluctantly, Grind accepted the call and brought the phone to his ear.

"Hey," Princess said tersely.

"What's up?" Grind replied. "You good?"

"Mm hm. Where you at?"

Fat Folks slowly lowered himself back onto his seat likely because his flabby gut could no longer tolerate the strain of sitting up. He watched Grind. Grind watched a passing Amazon delivery van. This was his first time ever receiving a regular phone call from Princess. She usually video called him. Thinking nothing of it, he tapped a roll of ash from his cigarette and shrugged his shoulders as if she could see him doing it.

"Just hittin' corners out south with one of the guys. Lookin' for them one niggas. You still at the club?"

"Nah, I'm on my way home. You got my car? Or did you already drop it off?"

"Parked it outside Aqua's crib."

Princess paused then. "You don't have anything to tell me?"

Grind puffed and blew a stream of smoke at his window as he eyed a passing jogger. He clenched and unclenched his teeth. Glanced over at Fat Folks and seriously contemplated putting a bullet through his skull. There was no way in hell he was going to allow Fat Folks to follow through on the plan to kill Princess Kelly.

"Nah," he said. "Why you ask me that?"

"No reason. Just asking. I'll call you back." Princess replied, and ended the call.

Two minutes later, Fat Folks was scratching at his crotch and Grind was reaching for the ashtray to smash out his cigarette when a Cook County Sheriff patrol car and four Chicago Police Department squad cars whipped onto Prospect Avenue and blocked them in. Grind's eyes got big. Exhaling his last breath of smoke, he swiped his pistol to the floor and raised his hands in surrender as a phalanx of uniformed police officers move in with their guns drawn.

Grind and Fat Folks were already handcuffed and seated in the back of a squad car when a blacked-out Mercedes Sprinter rounded the corner behind them. It was trailed by a black Escalade, two snow white Suburbans, a white Bugatti, and a white Rolls-Royce Cullivan. All six vehicles moved in perfect formation, almost like a presidential motorcade. The gates to Princess's driveway swung inward, the vehicles rolled inside, and the gates swung shut.

As Grind and Fat Folks sat silently in the rear of the cop car, Grind ground his teeth together and mentally chastised himself for not being straight forward with Princess.

"Shorty just got us locked up," Fat Folks griped. "On fo'nem. She the Jakes."

Grind responded with a sharp elbow to Fat Folks' ribcage. The blow made Fat Folks suck in a breath of air through his teeth and grimace in pain. He didn't say another word as the squad car they were seated in zoomed away from the curb.

Chapter 28

"Amanda Williams orchestrated the planting of a hundred thousand tulips on these connecting lots sometime last fall," thirty year old Harmonique Evans said as she sat with her arms crossed in the driver's seat of her brand new BMW XM plug-in hybrid SUV, staring out the window at the snow-laden vacant lot at the corner of East 53rd Street and South Prairie Avenue.

Baby Stone sat next to her in the passenger's seat. He'd put $150,000 of his own money toward the price of her $167,395 BMW. He also paid the full $341,899 for the nine carat Harry Winston engagement ring he'd presented to her on the eve of her last birthday, and he'd invested nearly a million dollars into Fleek Park, the high-end designer boutique she'd built just across the street from where the tulips would soon bloom again.

"It was a public project," Harmonique went on. "Over four hundred people helped her plant all those tulips. I snapped a few pictures of them last spring. They were so beautiful. So incredibly breathtaking. I framed one of those pics and hung it in my mama's living room. You know she used to babysit Amanda."

Baby Stone only nodded his head and glowered at a dark gray Chevy Silverado as it went cruising past Harmonique's window. Three of his boys were posted up on the sidewalk just ahead of them, their eyes peeled for any signs of danger. Six others were seated in the two luxury SUVs that were parked behind and in front of Harmonique's BMW, and Fleek Park's usual staff of eight men and women included two more members of Baby Stone's gang. They were the primary reason no one had committed any smash and grabs to the storefront windows.

Baby Stone picked up his smartphone and pulled up a list of available beachfront condominiums in Lido Key, an affluent stretch of paradise in Sarasota, Florida. He handed his phone to Harmonique and allowed her a long moment to peruse the listings before he spoke.

"So," he asked, "what you think?"

Harmonique's brow went high, and she went to reading about the newly constructed Rosewood Residences. The starting prices were in the six million dollar range, and that was for the two bedroom units. She had been trying to talk Baby Stone into moving south for months now. The gang violence in their Hyde Park neighborhood was bad, and lately it had begun to get a lot worse. Up until now, he'd never shown any real interest in leaving Chicago.

"Are you thinking of investing in one of these condos?" Harmonique asked, finally turning to look at him.

Baby Stone nodded his head. "I made some phone calls earlier. Found a realtor who could get us into one of those two bedroom units for $32,000 a month. We'll have to move fast if we want it."

Harmonique stared thoughtfully at the man with whom she'd fallen so hopelessly in love with. He was a rich street nigga, a high ranking gang leader, but he wasn't nearly as cold-hearted as he pretended to be. He was a respected member of one of the most dangerous street gangs the city of Chicago had ever birthed, but the years upon years of urban warfare he'd experienced had made him keenly aware of his own mortality. Harmonique had a strong feeling that the numerous shootings that had taken place in Hyde Park over the past week or so was the catalyst for his sudden decision to flee the city. His ex-girlfriend, Thick Doll had stopped by the boutique a few hours ago and warned Harmonique to keep an eye on her rearview mirror. Word on the street was that Baby Stone owed some guy named Markio a lot of money, and Markio was coming after him for it.

"I'm all in on leaving the city for a while," Harmonique said, "But there's a lot to be done here at the boutique. I'm having those new Panneton cameras installed all throughout the store next week. I just received Gucci's winter collection, and those Chanel bags have been selling like crazy. You might wanna hold off on making that move. At least until the end of January.

"Nah," Baby Stone nibbled at the center of his bottom lip. His calculating brown eyes locked onto the snow-white Rolls-Royce Phantom with darkly tinted windows that went cruising past Harmonique's window. "Nah, we might have to get outta here a whole lot sooner than that.

Harmonique returned the phone to Baby Stone's grasp and shifted in her seat to face him. She wore a strawberry red Celine Homme sweater over skintight black leather pants and white and red boots by the same high-end designer. Her real locs were braided down beneath a thirty inch long wig of silky blonde colored hair. She was a fair-skinned woman with perfectly round D-cup breasts, a twenty-five inch waistline, and hips that were forty-five inches around, the kind of black woman who, in the famous words of Queen Bey, had to jump to put jeans on.

She'd already been a well-established woman before the start of the relationship with Baby Stone; she was a fitness model with hundreds of thousands of social media followers and a keen eye for fashion. She and Baby Stone had gone to high school together, but they hadn't actually spoken at length until they crossed paths three years ago when she was walking from her Hyde Park townhouse to her favorite reading spot at Promontory Point. She had just purchased Wahida Clark's *Justify My Thug* and was eager to start reading it, but when she reached the place she'd began to think of as her personal reading tree, she'd found Baby Stone standing there with his iPhone in hand, recording video of his three young children swimming in the lake. That fatherly side of him had drawn her right in, and they hadn't parted ways since.

Looking forward, Harmonique eyed the tail-end of the Rolls-Royce and wondered who was inside of it. She thought of the Chicagoans she knew could afford it: G Herbo, Jennifer Hudson, Lil Durk, Anthony Davis, and Oprah Winfrey. Most of them resided in other states now, in affluent gated communities where the fear of gun violence wasn't nearly as overwhelming.

Harmonique was nodding her head, sucking her bottom lip, and preparing to tell Baby Stone that she would board a flight with him first thing Monday morning when the Rolls-Royce came to a screeching stop half a block away. In that same instant, she glimpsed two white SUVs in her sideview mirror, Jeep Grand Cherokees. The fast kind that all the big time rap stars had in their music videos. They slid to a halt in the intersection, the doors flew open, and a group of masked men leapt out holding Draco pistols with drum magazines and green laser beams, aiming and firing at the three men who were standing on the sidewalk two car lengths ahead of Harmonique's BMW.

Harmonique screamed and ducked low in her seat. Her natural gray eyes widened in fear as she looked over at Baby Stone, and she became even more afraid when she saw that his eyes were just as big as hers. He drew a Glock pistol from inside his pants and told her to stay in the car, then he shoved open his door and rushed out into the line of fire.

The gunshots were loud and thunderous, rapid fire explosions that made Harmonique cringe and shrink below her steering wheel. She squeezed her eyes shut and prayed to Allah. Baby Stone had left his door open, and when Harmonique opened her eyes she gasped, brought her hands up to cover her gaping mouth, and howled out a heart aching moan.

Baby Stone hadn't made it past his door. He was sprawled out on the snow sprinkled sidewalk in front of Fleek Park, and there was a tall brown-skinned man standing over him with a green bandana tied around the lower half of his head. The man pointed his Draco at Baby Stone's face and opened fire and the contents of Baby Stone's skull splashed across the concrete like a smashed can of tomato soup.

Chapter 29

"Nice place you have here," Alexus said, tilting her head back to look up at the high beamed ceilings as she and the others wandered into Princess and Kamari' oak floored living room.

"Reminds me of a seaside villa I recently purchased in the south of France."

She swung her head to look back at Princess. "Have you ever been to Toulon? Marseille? Nice?"

Princess shook her head no and cast a glance at Millionaire Marko. He'd just received a text message on one of the two iPhones he carried, and apparently it was good news. His mood seemed to brighten instantaneously. His subtle smile only widened a bit, but the glow in his eyes was clearly discernible, and the tension in his shoulders vanished. He chuckled twice. Nodded his head as if there was a Tay Keith beat playing in his ears.

"Blake and I dropped almost a hundred million dollars on that villa," Alexus said as she lowered her voluptuous rump onto an Egyptian leather sofa. "We have so many acres of land there in Toulon, and we're opening a high rise hotel in Marseille sometime next fall. I'll let you film an episode of your show there as soon as it opens."

"This woman is fucking rich," Kamari chipped in, her angelic voice brimming with excitement. "I'm telling you sis; You have to take this deal. If we go about this the right way, you could end up being bigger than the Kardashians."

Princess sat down on the opposite sofa, crossed her legs, and stared across her cocktail table at the wealthiest, most famous woman on the planet. Millionaire Markio and a dozen others entered the room and found seats on the sofas, the armchairs, and the two daybeds, but Princess kept her eyes on Alexus Costilla King. She didn't need to look over at Markio to see that he was staring right at her. Her periphery worked just fine. He sat two seats to the right of Alexus, sipping from his Styrofoam cup, strolling through messages and social media on his phones, but his eyes never left Princess's legs, and her mouth, and her small, delicate hands.

"So, what's the deal?" Princess asked, ignoring the persistent buzz of notifications from her own iPhone. "What kind of contract are you offering? Are we talking six figures? Seven figures?"

"For you," Alexus said, interlacing her manicured fingers over her knee, "I'm talking eight figures. Twelve million dollars for the first two seasons. I may only be able to guarantee six-figure deals for the rest of the cast, but they'll make millions from exposure. A show like this one will likely pull in thirty to forty million viewers per episode. Especially after the marketing blitz my mom and I have planned."

Princess turned to study the Zhu Jinshi oil on canvas painting that hung from her living room's east wall while she crunched the numbers in her head. The Mexican bodyguards that had ushered Alexus into the mansion spoke briefly with Aqua and Kamari, and then they began escorting most of the others out of the room. Leaving only Kamari, Aqua, Princess, Markio, Alexus and Bojo, the hugely muscular Mexican man who for the past year or so had acted as Alexus primary bodyguard.

Following the tense moment of thoughtful silence, Alexus stood and crossed the room to stand before the expensive abstract painting. She spent a short time admiring its magnificent burst of color, running her fingertips over the rough edges. Then she turned and motioned for Princess to join her. Princess got up and walked over to stand beside the stunningly beautiful young billionaire, checking the notifications on her phone as she went. She had to force herself to remain stone-faced as she read the news that Baby Stone and several others had just been gunned down outside his fiancée's boutique on 53rd and Prairie. She had well over forty new text messages from her family and friends in Hyde Park, and every one of them was about the shooting. She halfway suspected there might be a connection between Baby Stone's murder and the positive shift in Millionaire Markio's disposition, and a part of her wondered if the men she'd seen in the other three white vehicles, the Rolls-Royce Phantom, and the two Jeep Grand Cherokee Trailhawks that had sped off in another direction as they were leaving the Queen of Diamonds parking lot were responsible for the murders.

"Stop using those Secure Force bodyguards," Alexus whispered. "They're essentially a secret branch of the Chicago Police Department. An actual CPD lieutenant runs the company, and they're known for investigating black celebrities. Keep them away from everyone in your circle."

Princess nodded her head and said nothing. For a while she and Alexus stood shoulder to shoulder, studying the painting in complete silence, while behind them Kamari and Aqua busied themselves asking Markio a hundred and one questions about his upcoming movie series.

"I heard about what you did to those boys out south earlier today," Alexus said a minute later. "I'm so proud of you. It takes real guts to do something like that. I'll never forget my first murder." She snickered quietly. "That was so many murders ago."

Princess furrowed her brow in confusion, but again she remained silent.

"I FaceTimed with Weezy on the way here," Alexus went on. "I believe he feels some type of way about Markio's ties to Baby Stone, but from what I understand, Baby Stone's no longer a threat, and Markio ran the old man Herb out of town. Everything should be good with you and your friend over there continuing to dance at Queen of Diamonds. Weezy's in it for the money, and he knows how much business he'll get from a hit reality show starring his most prized dancers. I made it clear that you'll be in charge of things, and that it would be in his best interest to keep you happy. If anything comes up, just give me a call."

Princess exhaled a huge sigh of relief. She scissored her legs and folded her arms over her chest. Stuck out her lower lip. Rubbed an elbow, adjusted the diamond hoop in her left earlobe. She had slipped into her bedroom shortly after arriving at her palatial mansion, to step into a tight pair if black Louis Vuitton sweatpants and tuck her Glock behind her waistline, and she still had on the purple laced Fenty bra she'd put on for the dance audition. Her palms were sweaty. She wiped them on her thighs and took another deep breath, contemplating the possible ramifications of Baby Stone's death. The south side of Chicago would be dangerous place for the next couple of months; of this she was certain. The North Lawndale neighborhood, Millionaire Markio's stomping grounds would undoubtedly have its fair share of murders as well, but Princess didn't have anything to do with the streets. She danced on the pole and then came home to her daughter, and now she had a television deal on the table, a deal that guaranteed her a twelve million dollar payday. She'd be able to afford security, and if things went bad with Weezy and his crew of Gangster Disciples, she'd be able to pay the Black P. Stones she grew up around to put all of them six feet underground. She'd hire bodyguards from another security firm to take her everywhere she needed to go, and if anyone played crazy, there would be hell to pay.

"Okay," she said to Alexus. "I'm in. Have someone bring me the paperwork and send that money to my bank account. And don't forget about that million dollars you promised me on top of that twelve million."

Alexus snickered again. "You're my kind of girl," she said, and wrapped her arm around Princess shoulders. "We're gonna make a lot of money together. Mark my words."

Epilogue
February 18, 2024

It was a warm, sunny evening in Miami Beach, Florida, and Herbert Harris was in the very best of moods. Dressed in a black Balenciaga tracksuit and New Balance sneakers, his wrist adorned with a yellow-gold Rolex Sky-Dweller, Herb sat in a sumptuous off-white leather armchair with his feet kicked up on a matching ottoman, rolling a small blue Viagra pill between his thumb and forefinger while watching his two chocolate goddesses lick and suck on each other's juicy pink pussies. They were on the king-size bed next to his chair, Tiffany on top with her back arched and her glistening wet vaginal lips hovering an inch above Tylisha's extended tongue. Two of Tylisha's fingers were deep in Tiffany's asshole. Her chin and mouth were drenched. The flawless white diamond Chanel bracelet she wore on her right wrist had cost Herb more than twenty grand.

The three of them were in the master bedroom suite of an 18,000 square foot mansion on Star Island, the exclusive Miami Beach enclave where Rick Ross, Jennifer Lopez, and pharmaceutical billionaire, Phillip Frost were among past and present residents. The NBA All-Star game was playing on the enormous ninety inch smart TV, but Herb was having a hard time paying attention.

It wasn't the girls that had him so unfocused; both of them had already sucked, jerked, and ridden his dick until several geysers of gooey white semen spurted out of him, just as they'd done every day for the past couple of months. Now, it was Millionaire Markio who had the old man's full attention. Herb was 81 now, and as one would expect, there were a lot of memories that had burned away with age, but there were certain indelible memories that would never go away. One of them was the hellfire Herb had seen in the wealthy young novelist's eyes when he met up with Herb on the front porch of the Hillside home Herb's wife had lived in for the past 53 years. Markio and four of his henchmen had climbed the porch steps with a purpose, making no effort to conceal the miniature assault rifles they'd held in their hands.

"Stay the fuck outta my b'ness, old school," Markio had threatened. *"This the only warning you gon' get. Baby Stone wanna be a gangsta. As soon as my shooters catch him outside, they gon' show him what it means to be a gangsta. And if I hear one more word about you tryna extort Weezy with that video, your old ass is gon' end up just like your nephew. We clear on that?"*

Herb had hesitated, and Markio had raised his Draco and pressed the barrel against Herb's jaw before repeating the question.

"We're clear," Herb had replied reluctantly.

Now thinking back to that blistering cold December afternoon and the many dark days that had followed, the intense heartache of attending Baby Stone's funeral, and having to watch Harmonique and the mothers of Baby Stone's children cry their eyes out over his closed casket, the ensuing shootouts between the Hyde Park Black P. Stones and the Holy City Vice Lords. The tearful nights Herb had spent reminiscing over the memory of his deceased nephew while nursing a bottle of the finest whiskey money could buy, Herb could think of only one thing. Revenge.

Herb's wife, Lynette "Bone" Harris, was Markio's mother's oldest sister. Bone's nephew had taken out Herb's nephew, and now Herb was going to make sure his wife experienced that same unbearable pain.

He snapped out of his reverie when Tiffany threw her head back and let out an ear-piercing moan. Tylisha wrapped her arms around Tiffany's waist, sealing her mouth around Tiffany's clitoris as a burst of transparent vaginal juices squirted out of her. The arousing sight of Tiffany's orgasm had a notable effect on Herb. He licked his lips, flared his nostrils and inhaled deeply placing the little blue pill on the tip of his tongue and swallowed it down. He was picking up the TV remote to mute the sound and join the girls in bed when he spotted someone sitting courtside at the All-Star game. He narrowed his eyes, leaned forward in his chair, digging his age-spotted fingers into the leather really focusing in.

Tiffany toppled over next to Tylisha, giggling in the wake of her orgasm. Tylisha sat up, wiped her mouth, and shot a glance at the television.

"You saw him too, didn't you?" Tylisha asked, looking at Herb.

Herb only nodded. He wasn't sure who he'd seen, but the man had certainly looked familiar.

"That was Millionaire Markio and Princess Kelly," Tylisha said, rising up onto her knees. "You know they're dating now. I saw it on the second episode of her show. The third episode airs tonight."

Herb wrinkled his brow and continued watching the game. The camera panned left, following Lebron James as he sprinted down court and rose up for a dunk. This time Herb got a good look at Markio. The man was light brown in complexion, just like his Aunt Bone, and all her siblings. He had two teardrops inked beside his left eye, and he wore a bold yellow Louis Vuitton sweater over his designer jeans and Air Jordan sneakers. His gaudy accessories included a pair of Cartier sunglasses with white diamonds sprinkled across the nose bridge, four or five white diamond necklaces, and a chunky white diamond watch. The woman seated next to him was the pure epitome of Africa American female beauty, with rich brown skin, full glossed lips, and an equally icy watch encircling he left wrist. She had on a black tee with a photo of Beyonce printed on the chest and tight fitting black leather pants over Louboutin heels, a black croc-skin Hermes Birkin handbag rested next to her left shoe, and her eyes were tucked away behind dark Chanel shades. Her Cuban link necklace had her diamond encrusted name hanging down from it. She possessed the natural kind of beauty Tifany and Tylisha would never have, no matter how much cash Herb threw their way. She was stunning, she was curvy, and if there was one black woman on earth with more sex appeal than Princess Kelly, Herb had yet to lay eyes on her. He hadn't seen he since his nephew's funeral, and it had only been for a couple of minutes, but she'd stolen the show then just as she was doing now.

Herb shifted his gaze to Tylisha. Handing her the remote he said, "Pull up that TV show she's on. I wanna see what's going on between her and Markio."

"It's called The Real Bad Bitches of Chicago," Tiffany said. "It's the hottest new reality show on TV. Princess just found out that Markio

and Bunny used to date or whatever, and she got into a whole fight with Bunny over the shit. She threw a Dussé bottle at Bunny's head. Kimmy and Thick Doll jumped in to help Princess, then Cherish and Shmoney jumped in to help Bunny. It went up. I can't wait to see that third episode."

Tylisha took all of twenty seconds to switch from the All-Star game to the MTN streaming app. By then, Herb's growing erection had turned the front of his pants into a tent. Tylisha slipped down from the bed and sashayed over to him, helping him back to the seat in the armchair and yanking down his pants and underwear in one swift motion. She kneeled between his parted legs and took him into her soothingly warm mouth, while Herb stared fixedly at the smart television across the room from him.

In that moment, Herbert Harris became one of the fifty million viewers who'd tuned in to watch the first two episodes of black America's favorite new reality TV series, though his interest in the show had nothing to do with the petty disputes and histrionic rants of its jaw dropping attractive cast members, nor did he have an interest in their provocative pole dances. Herb's only reason for watching the show was to keep an eye on Princess Kelly and the man he was certain hand ordered Baby Stone's murder.

As Tylisha's noisily wet mouth began sliding up and down the length of Herb's erection, he kept himself from ejaculating prematurely by focusing on the mission ahead of him. Soon, he told himself, he would hunt down Millionaire Markio and slit his throat before he could even think to reach for his gun. If Princess was with Markio when Herb caught up with him, then she too would perish.

It was only a matter of time…

TO BE CONTINUED

Lock Down Publications and Ca$h Presents
Assisted Publishing Packages

BASIC PACKAGE	UPGRADED PACKAGE
$499	$800
Editing	Typing
Cover Design	Editing
Formatting	Cover Design
	Formatting
ADVANCE PACKAGE	**LDP SUPREME PACKAGE**
$1,200	$1,500
Typing	Typing
Editing	Editing
Cover Design	Cover Design
Formatting	Formatting
Copyright registration	Copyright registration
Proofreading	Proofreading
Upload book to Amazon	Set up Amazon account
	Upload book to Amazon
	Advertise on LDP, Amazon and Facebook Page

***Other services available upon request.
Additional charges may apply

Lock Down Publications
P.O. Box 944
Stockbridge, GA 30281-9998
Phone: 470 303-9761

Submission Guideline

Submit the first three chapters of your completed manuscript to ldpsubmissions@gmail.com. In the subject line add **Your Book's Title**. The manuscript must be in a Word Doc file and sent as an attachment. Document should be in Times New Roman, double spaced, and in size 12 font. Also, provide your synopsis and full contact information. If sending multiple submissions, they must each be in a separate email.

Have a story but no way to send it electronically? You can still submit to LDP/Ca$h Presents. Send in the first three chapters, written or typed, of your completed manuscript to:

LDP: Submissions Dept
P.O. Box 944
Stockbridge, GA 30281-9998

DO NOT send original manuscript. Must be a duplicate. Provide your synopsis and a cover letter containing your full contact information.

Thanks for considering LDP and Ca$h Presents.

NEW RELEASES

BLOODLINE OF A SAVAGE 1&2
THESE VICIOUS STREETS
RELENTLESS GOON
RELENTLESS GOON 2
BY PRINCE A. TAUHID

THE BUTTERFLY MAFIA 1-3
BY FUMIYA PAYNE

A THUG'S STREET PRINCESS 1&2
BY MEESHA

CITY OF SMOKE 2
BY MOLOTTI

STEPPERS 1,2&3
BY KING RIO

THE LANE 1&2
BY KEN-KEN SPENCE

THUG OF SPADES 1&2
LOVE IN THE TRENCHES 2
BY COREY ROBINSON

TIL DEATH 3
BY ARYANNA

THE BIRTH OF A GANGSTER 4
BY DELMONT PLAYER

PRODUCT OF THE STREETS 1&2
BY DEMOND "MONEY" ANDERSON

NO TIME FOR ERROR
BY KEESE

MONEY HUNGRY DEMONS
BY TRANAY ADAMS

Coming Soon from Lock Down Publications/Ca$h Presents

IF YOU CROSS ME ONCE 6
ANGEL V
By Anthony Fields

IMMA DIE BOUT MINE 4&5
By Aryanna

A THUGS STREET PRINCESS 3
By Meesha

PRODUCT OF THE STREETS 3
By Demond Money Anderson

CORNER BOYS
By Corey Robinson

SON OF A DOPE FIEND 4
By Renta

THE MURDER QUEENS 6&7
By Michael Gallon

CITY OF SMOKE 3
By Molotti

BETRAYAL OF A G
By Ray Vinci

CONFESSIONS OF A DOPE BOY
By Nicholas Lock

THA TAKEOVER
By Keith Chandler

Available Now

RESTRAINING ORDER 1 & 2
By **CA$H & Coffee**

LOVE KNOWS NO BOUNDARIES 1-3
By **Coffee**

RAISED AS A GOON I, II, III & IV
BRED BY THE SLUMS I, II, III
BLAST FOR ME I & II
ROTTEN TO THE CORE I II III
A BRONX TALE I, II, III
DUFFLE BAG CARTEL I II III IV V VI
HEARTLESS GOON I II III IV V
A SAVAGE DOPEBOY I II
DRUG LORDS I II III
CUTTHROAT MAFIA I II
KING OF THE TRENCHES
By **Ghost**

LAY IT DOWN I & II
LAST OF A DYING BREED I II
BLOOD STAINS OF A SHOTTA I & II III
By **Jamaica**

LOYAL TO THE GAME I II III
LIFE OF SIN I, II III
By **TJ & Jelissa**

IF LOVING HIM IS WRONG…I & II
LOVE ME EVEN WHEN IT HURTS I II III
By **Jelissa**

BLOODY COMMAS I & II
SKI MASK CARTEL I, II & III
KING OF NEW YORK I II, III IV V
RISE TO POWER I II III
COKE KINGS I II III IV V
BORN HEARTLESS I II III IV
KING OF THE TRAP I II
By **T.J. Edwards**

WHEN THE STREETS CLAP BACK I & II III
THE HEART OF A SAVAGE I II III IV
MONEY MAFIA I II
LOYAL TO THE SOIL I II III
By **Jibril Williams**

A DISTINGUISHED THUG STOLE MY HEART I II &
III
LOVE SHOULDN'T HURT I II III IV
RENEGADE BOYS 1-4
PAID IN KARMA 1-3
SAVAGE STORMS 1-3
AN UNFORESEEN LOVE 1-3
BABY, I'M WINTERTIME COLD 1-3
A THUG'S STREET PRINCESS 1&2
By **Meesha**

A GANGSTER'S CODE 1-3
A GANGSTER'S SYN 1-3
THE SAVAGE LIFE 1-3
CHAINED TO THE STREETS 1-3
BLOOD ON THE MONEY 1-3
A GANGSTA'S PAIN 1-3
BEAUTIFUL LIES AND UGLY TRUTHS
CHURCH IN THESE STREETS
By **J-Blunt**

PUSH IT TO THE LIMIT
By **Bre' Hayes**

BLOOD OF A BOSS 1-5
SHADOWS OF THE GAME
TRAP BASTARD
By **Askari**

THE STREETS BLEED MURDER 1-3
THE HEART OF A GANGSTA 1-3
By **Jerry Jackson**

CUM FOR ME 1-8
An LDP Erotica Collaboration

BRIDE OF A HUSTLA 1-3
THE FETTI GIRLS 1-3
CORRUPTED BY A GANGSTA 1-4
BLINDED BY HIS LOVE
THE PRICE YOU PAY FOR LOVE 1-3
DOPE GIRL MAGIC 1-3
By **Destiny Skai**

WHEN A GOOD GIRL GOES BAD
By **Adrienne**

A KINGPIN'S AMBITION
A KINGPIN'S AMBITION II
I MURDER FOR THE DOUGH
By **Ambitious**

THE COST OF LOYALTY 1-3
By **Kweli**

A GANGSTER'S REVENGE 1-4
THE BOSS MAN'S DAUGHTERS 1-5
A SAVAGE LOVE 1&2
BAE BELONGS TO ME 1&2
A HUSTLER'S DECEIT 1-3
WHAT BAD BITCHES DO 1-3
SOUL OF A MONSTER 1-3
KILL ZONE
A DOPE BOY'S QUEEN 1-3
TIL DEATH 1-3
IMMA DIE BOUT MINE 1-3
By **Aryanna**

TRUE SAVAGE 1-7
DOPE BOY MAGIC 1-3
MIDNIGHT CARTEL 1-3
CITY OF KINGZ 1&2
NIGHTMARE ON SILENT AVE
THE PLUG OF LIL MEXICO 1&2
CLASSIC CITY
By **Chris Green**

A DOPEBOY'S PRAYER
By **Eddie "Wolf" Lee**

THE KING CARTEL 1-3
By **Frank Gresham**

THESE NIGGAS AIN'T LOYAL 1-3
By **Nikki Tee**

GANGSTA SHYT 1-3
By **CATO**

THE ULTIMATE BETRAYAL
By **Phoenix**

BOSS'N UP 1-3
By **Royal Nicole**

I LOVE YOU TO DEATH
By **Destiny J**

I RIDE FOR MY HITTA
I STILL RIDE FOR MY HITTA
By **Misty Holt**

LOVE & CHASIN' PAPER
By **Qay Crockett**

TO DIE IN VAIN
SINS OF A HUSTLA
By **ASAD**

BROOKLYN HUSTLAZ
By **Boogsy Morina**

BROOKLYN ON LOCK 1 & 2
By **Sonovia**

GANGSTA CITY
By T**eddy Duke**

A DRUG KING AND HIS DIAMOND 1-3
A DOPEMAN'S RICHES
HER MAN, MINE'S TOO 1&2
CASH MONEY HO'S
THE WIFEY I USED TO BE 1&2
PRETTY GIRLS DO NASTY THINGS
By **Nicole Goosby**

LIPSTICK KILLAH 1-3
CRIME OF PASSION 1-3
FRIEND OR FOE 1-3
By **Mimi**

TRAPHOUSE KING 1-3
KINGPIN KILLAZ 1-3
STREET KINGS 1&2
PAID IN BLOOD 1&2
CARTEL KILLAZ 1-3
DOPE GODS 1&2
By **Hood Rich**

STEADY MOBBN' 1-3
THE STREETS STAINED MY SOUL 1-3
By **Marcellus Allen**

WHO SHOT YA 1-3
SON OF A DOPE FIEND 1-3
HEAVEN GOT A GHETTO 1&2
SKI MASK MONEY 1&2
By **Renta**

GORILLAZ IN THE BAY 1-4
TEARS OF A GANGSTA 1/&2
3X KRAZY 1&2
STRAIGHT BEAST MODE 1&2
By **DE'KARI**

TRIGGADALE 1-3
MURDA WAS THE CASE 1-3
By **Elijah R. Freeman**

THE STREETS ARE CALLING
By **Duquie Wilson**

SLAUGHTER GANG 1-3
RUTHLESS HEART 1-3
By **Willie Slaughter**

GOD BLESS THE TRAPPERS 1-3
THESE SCANDALOUS STREETS 1-3
FEAR MY GANGSTA 1-5
THESE STREETS DON'T LOVE NOBODY 1-2
BURY ME A G 1-5
A GANGSTA'S EMPIRE 1-4
THE DOPEMAN'S BODYGAURD 1&2
THE REALEST KILLAZ 1-3
THE LAST OF THE OGS 1-3
By **Tranay Adams**

MARRIED TO A BOSS 1-3
By **Destiny Skai & Chris Green**

KINGZ OF THE GAME 1-7
CRIME BOSS 1-3
By **Playa Ray**

FUK SHYT
By **Blakk Diamond**

DON'T F#CK WITH MY HEART 1&2
By **Linnea**

ADDICTED TO THE DRAMA 1-3
IN THE ARM OF HIS BOSS
By **Jamila**

LOYALTY AIN'T PROMISED 1&2
By **Keith Williams**

YAYO 1-4
A SHOOTER'S AMBITION 1&2
BRED IN THE GAME
By **S. Allen**

TRAP GOD 1-3
RICH $AVAGE 1-3
MONEY IN THE GRAVE 1-3
CARTEL MONEY
By **Martell Troublesome Bolden**

FOREVER GANGSTA 1&2
GLOCKS ON SATIN SHEETS 1&2
By **Adrian Dulan**

TOE TAGZ 1-4
LEVELS TO THIS SHYT 1&2
IT'S JUST ME AND YOU
By **Ah'Million**

KINGPIN DREAMS 1-3
RAN OFF ON DA PLUG
By **Paper Boi Rari**

CONFESSIONS OF A GANGSTA 1-4
CONFESSIONS OF A JACKBOY 1-3
CONFESSIONS OF A HITMAN
By **Nicholas Lock**

I'M NOTHING WITHOUT HIS LOVE
SINS OF A THUG
TO THE THUG I LOVED BEFORE
A GANGSTA SAVED XMAS
IN A HUSTLER I TRUST
By **Monet Dragun**

QUIET MONEY 1-3
THUG LIFE 1-3
EXTENDED CLIP 1&2
A GANGSTA'S PARADISE
By **Trai'Quan**

CAUGHT UP IN THE LIFE 1-3
THE STREETS NEVER LET GO 1-3
By **Robert Baptiste**

NEW TO THE GAME 1-3
MONEY, MURDER & MEMORIES 1-3
By **Malik D. Rice**

CREAM 2-3
THE STREETS WILL TALK
By **Yolanda Moore**

LIFE OF A SAVAGE 1-4
A GANGSTA'S QUR'AN 1-4
MURDA SEASON 1-3
GANGLAND CARTEL 1-3
CHI'RAQ GANGSTAS 1-4
KILLERS ON ELM STREET 1-3
JACK BOYZ N DA BRONX 1-3
A DOPEBOY'S DREAM 1-3
JACK BOYS VS DOPE BOYS 1-3
COKE GIRLZ
COKE BOYS
SOSA GANG 1&2
BRONX SAVAGES
BODYMORE KINGPINS
BLOOD OF A GOON
By **Romell Tukes**

THE STREETS MADE ME 1-3
By **Larry D. Wright**

CONCRETE KILLA 1-3
VICIOUS LOYALTY 1-3
By **Kingpen**

THE ULTIMATE SACRIFICE 1-6
KHADIFI
IF YOU CROSS ME ONCE 1-3
ANGEL 1-4
IN THE BLINK OF AN EYE
By **Anthony Fields**

THE LIFE OF A HOOD STAR
By **Ca$h & Rashia Wilson**

THE STREETS WILL NEVER CLOSE 1-3
By **K'ajji**

NIGHTMARES OF A HUSTLA 1-3
By **King Dream**

HARD AND RUTHLESS 1&2
MOB TOWN 251
THE BILLIONAIRE BENTLEYS 1-3
REAL G'S MOVE IN SILENCE
By **Von Diesel**

GHOST MOB
By **Stilloan Robinson**

MOB TIES 1-6
SOUL OF A HUSTLER, HEART OF A KILLER 1-3
GORILLAZ IN THE TRENCHES
By **SayNoMore**

BODYMORE MURDERLAND 1-3
THE BIRTH OF A GANGSTER 1-4
By **Delmont Player**

FOR THE LOVE OF A BOSS 1&2
By **C. D. Blue**

KILLA KOUNTY 1-5
By **Khufu**

MOBBED UP 1-4
THE BRICK MAN 1-5
THE COCAINE PRINCESS 1-10
STEPPERS 1-3
SUPER GREMLIN 1-4
By **King Rio**

MONEY GAME 1&2
By **Smoove Dolla**

A GANGSTA'S KARMA 1-4
By **FLAME**

KING OF THE TRENCHES 1-3
By **GHOST & TRANAY ADAMS**

QUEEN OF THE ZOO 1&2
By **Black Migo**

GRIMEY WAYS 1-3
By **Ray Vinci**

XMAS WITH AN ATL SHOOTER
By **Ca$h & Destiny Skai**

THE REAL BADDIES OF CHI-RAQ | KING RIO

KING KILLA 1&2
By **Vincent "Vitto" Holloway**

BETRAYAL OF A THUG 1&2
By **Fre$h**

THE MURDER QUEENS 1-5
By **Michael Gallon**

FOR THE LOVE OF BLOOD 1-4
By **Jamel Mitchell**

HOOD CONSIGLIERE 1&2
NO TIME FOR ERROR
By **Keese**

PROTÉGÉ OF A LEGEND 1&2
LOVE IN THE TRENCHES 1&2
By **Corey Robinson**

BORN IN THE GRAVE 1-3
CRIME PAYS
By **Self Made Tay**

MOAN IN MY MOUTH
By **XTASY**

TORN BETWEEN A GANGSTER AND A GENTLEMAN
By **J-BLUNT & Miss Kim**

LOYALTY IS EVERYTHING 1-3
CITY OF SMOKE 1&2
By **Molotti**

HERE TODAY GONE TOMORROW 1&2
By **Fly Rock**

WOMEN LIE MEN LIE 1-4
FIFTY SHADES OF SNOW 1-3
STACK BEFORE YOU SPLURGE
GIRLS FALL LIKE DOMINOES
NAÏVE TO THE STREETS
By **ROY MILLIGAN**

PILLOW PRINCESS
By **S. Hawkins**

THE BUTTERFLY MAFIA 1-3
SALUTE MY SAVAGERY 1&2
By **Fumiya Payne**

THE LANE 1&2
By Ken-Ken Spence

THE PUSSY TRAP 1-5
By **Nene Capri**

DIRTY DNA
By **Blaque**

SANCTIFIED AND HORNY
by **XTASY**

BOOKS BY LDP'S CEO, CA$H

TRUST IN NO MAN
TRUST IN NO MAN 2
TRUST IN NO MAN 3
BONDED BY BLOOD
SHORTY GOT A THUG
THUGS CRY
THUGS CRY 2
THUGS CRY 3
TRUST NO BITCH
TRUST NO BITCH 2
TRUST NO BITCH 3
TIL MY CASKET DROPS
RESTRAINING ORDER
RESTRAINING ORDER 2
IN LOVE WITH A CONVICT
LIFE OF A HOOD STAR
XMAS WITH AN ATL SHOOTER